I0626173

RANDOM JACK

TALES FROM JAZZTOWN & BEYOND

BY JACK RANDOM

CROW DOG PRESS
TURLOCK CA USA

Random Jack:

Tales from Jazztown & Beyond

By Jack Random

Published by
Crow Dog Press
1241 Windsor Court
Turlock CA 95380

Copyright 2016 Ray Miller

All rights reserved. No part of this book may be reproduced in any form or by any means, electronic or mechanical, including photocopying, recording, or by any information storage and retrieval system, without permission in writing from the publisher.

Cover art adapted from "Express Yourself" by Nina Mera 1994 oil on canvas.

ISBN-13: 978-0997788310
ISBN-10: 0997788313

RANDOM JACK

Tales from Jazztown & Beyond

BY

JACK RANDOM

FORWARD

As a writer and a human being, Jack Random is an enigma. He personifies the duality of man. His bloodline runs through Oklahoma, aka Indian Territory, where the Trail of Tears once ended, where the European invaders crossed paths and intermarried with the Apache, Cherokee, Arapaho, Chickasaw, Black Feet and Lakota.

The offspring of an Idaho sharecropper and a California pugilist, he has at times felt equally at home sitting around a fire circle or a poker table, in a sweat lodge or jazz joint, in the heart of a bustling city or in the isolation of a great southwest desert. He is a quiet man with a restless spirit. He is a spiritual man whose religious beliefs are grounded in mother earth.

Jack Random is many things and yet he is none of these. He is a writer and therefore he is what he writes. In the end it may be that we can never truly know another human being. We know what we gather through the senses. We know the observable, the persona or the exterior of an individual without depth or shading. We know the mythology of a man. We get no more than a glimpse of the great mystery that is everyman or everywoman.

Jack Random is a writer. He is what he writes. Nothing more. Nothing less.

The pieces in this collection date back to 1996-97 when *Random Erotica* and *Tales from Jazztown* were published in handbook form. Asked for his comments, noted poet-musician-artist Jake Berry wrote:

"There be saints of the native soil here, and Christ what a story: Our visionary slashed by seductive wench, our souls abandoned in timeless cinema of souls – all soul's night howling at me from the page!"

America's Intercultural Magazine (AIM) originally published Burning Churches. *Lynx Eye* published Wild Man of Albuquerque and Fatal Flaw. The Trumpet Player and The Torch Singer were published in *Mobius*.

TABLE OF CONTENTS

ILLUSTRATIONS

TALES FROM JAZZTOWN

WELCOME TO JAZZTOWN

Those who come to Jazztown are driven though they may drive alone. Once they enter the gates they are bound for the duration. Here there are interwoven tales of disparate and desperate souls that awaken at midnight and find themselves trapped, unable to shake the visions and dreams that claw and scratch from the marrow of their bones. They yield as they must yield. They have no choice. They are welcomed with open arms and open thighs, open hearts and minds. Here they are free to live out their destinies, secure in the knowledge that what happens here is not real. It cannot be and yet it is.

A cold sweat invades the calm of idle muses as sweet jazz filters through clouds of smoke, soothing the rankled soul. What is the illusion: The vision or the photograph, the dream or sensation, the shadow or the light? In Jazztown there are no parameters of time and space. There is no code of morality. There is only the beat, the rhythm and the feel of jazz.

Rhythm and blues, honky tonk, bebop, scat jazz and the torch singer. Everything is black and white in endless shades of gray. Every corner holds a diner, every block a jazz joint, every man and woman a story and a dream. For the cost of a whiskey or a cup of coffee they'll tell you all about it. For the same price they'll listen to yours.

There's a rich cat charading as a street poet. Be careful what you dream. There's an endless chain of drunken wet dream fantasies. Be careful where you roam. There's a horn man in search of Charlie Parker's soul. There's a writer who pens himself into an asylum of oblivion. There's a torchbearer who lights a flame in every heart but her own. Be careful what you wish. The jazzman is plotting sweet revenge and the stripper of fashion becomes the stripper of souls. And then there's you.

"What brings you to these parts?" the old man laughs, his toothless orifice resonating with mirth. As if he didn't know. Be careful what you dream.

PARADISE BAR

Decked in Johnny-Be-Good patent leather soles, double breast and padded shoulder zoot, tilted gangster slick in black, he turned the corner and strutted down the cobblestone alleyway at dusk. Inside the bar a cat in tan loafers, cool and wrinkle free despite beads of wilted sweat on his pale and lifeless brow, eyed the unattended redhead once or twice too much.

He couldn't help but notice
As he scanned the local clime
There was murder in the air that night
There was murder on his mind

"What's shakin' Red?" He ordered up a brew. She gave a glance, that's all it took; he gave the cat a second look. She lifted her glass: Here's to you, stranger. As long as you're here you might as well put down a few.

He drank his last and left the bar but he never made to his car. Jack followed to explain.

There's murder in the air my friend
And murder is your end...

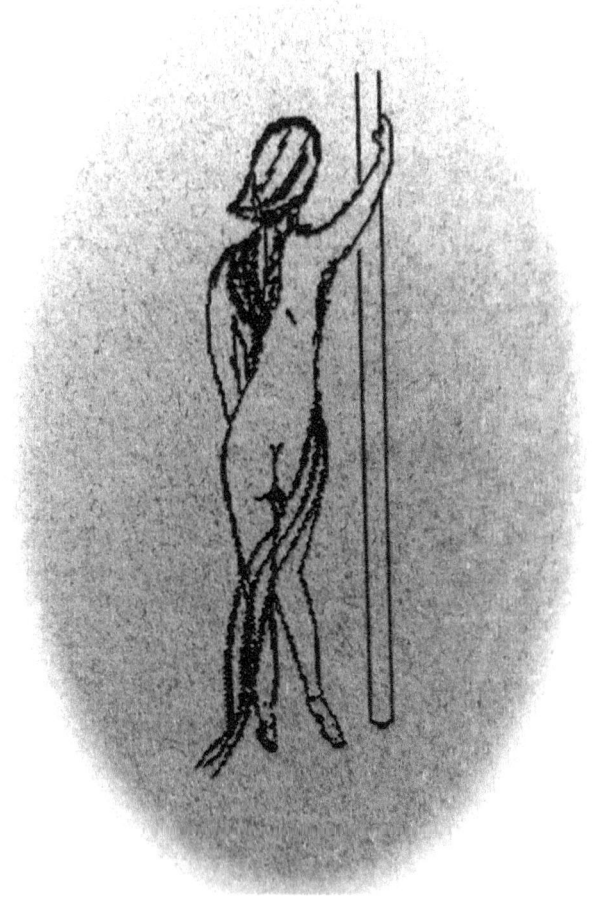

Jazz Dancer

JAZZ DANCER

She was the prized creation of another world
Where movement was slow and sensual
And dance was second nature

She coasted over the stage
Painting circles with her grace
And coiled round the metal phallus like a snake

The casual elegance with which she bared her private
Beauty released all sense of shame
And left them green with envy
Shaken with desire

She gave them dreams of pleasure
And accepted their gratuity

SWEET RUBY

Jack sat back to the wall and fed his reflection to the last Jack Daniels of the evening. Or so he thought until sweet Ruby graced his weary sight, a wink and a nod and a promise of delight.

"Mind if I?"

No, I don't, he said with his brows as she sat herself beside him, letting her parted skirt fly, revealing a red rose beneath black fishnet stockings.

"The night is just beginning to get interesting."

He liked the sound of her voice, the pull in her eyes, the tilt in his loins, and angled for a better view.

She purred like a cat, barely parting her lips: "You like what you see?"

"Does a tick like dogs?" he thought, and panted his reply.

"If you're still here in thirty seconds, it's all yours, big guy."

She winked and strolled to the bar; his eyes trailed behind her, begging for a clue. But before he had a moment to think it through a man the size of a grizzly with the face to match was dragging his chains toward him with the thump of heavy leather. He bulldozed the table and reached for Jack's throat.

Jack rescued what remained of his whiskey and tossed it in the monster's eyes, buying time to plant his knee where the seeds of little monsters waited to be planted. Startled but undaunted the beast laughed a hearty growl.

Balls of steel, thought Jack, and braced for his demise.

The beast took a liking to him and spared him too much pain. He only broke his nose and a gave him a thumping escort out the door.

Jack managed to sit upright on the curb and thought beneath the sweat and blood of his dwindling desire: Interesting. She's not even my type.

He didn't bother to dust himself off and announced to no one listening.

"A man's got to put it on the line every once in a while, even if it costs a whiskey."

If he had a drink, he'd have made a toast. Instead, he struggled to his feet and called it a night.

WANING LIGHT

Iridescent in the waning light
She descended the winding staircase
Like a divine being or a vision heaven sent
She graced my soul

An older woman in the fall of life
Her earthly beauty consensus held
Past its portent bloom
Yet for a moment she held before my eyes
The beauty of a thousand wet dreams fulfilled
And my love moved to her
And hers encompassed mine
And ours enveloped humankind

EVERYTHING IS TIME

She is a leathered goddess of the lower eastside
Motorcycle mama with her knees apart
Inciting wet dreams and animal instincts
Her leather squeezing tight caressing my desire

She shoots a knowing glance my way
Forming words none can hear but me:
You're mine for the taking

Squirm and feel the pulsing heat of primal urge
Streaming from the black hole of no tomorrow
I refuse to wag my tongue and straighten
My cool in the reflection of a bottle

Her lips move: Give it a shot
What have you got to lose?

Nothing, I answered by rote
    Nothing but my soul

Like a snake drawn to shadow I slither to her table
And stand like a dumbstruck boy without words
It'll cost you she purrs
I know, I reply, how much?
How long, she answers.
    Everything is time.

I empty my pockets
Not here, friend, she smiles

JACK RANDOM

I don't do this for anyone

I lower myself as commoner to queen
What's the deal? I inquire.

She touches my hand with the tips of her fingers
To remind me of her power

    You can look but don't touch

I smile in submission
She knows I want more but this will do
    It will have to

She tightens her hold and seals her sacred bond
Strutting without another word to the door
Hips dancing like waves of moonlight on black velvet

Once more into the streets
The barren lonely soulful streets of the lower eastside

Vanished without a trace
Another drunken wet dream fantasy
On the streets of Jazztown

THE TORCH SINGER

She told herself it didn't matter. A roll of the dice. One too many snake eyes in the craps of life. She told herself it would make her stronger. She told herself it was destiny. In another life she'd been a thug, a dealer, a dirty businessman, a hustler or a pimp. Now she paid the price. It would give her depth of character. It would give her soul. It would make her a better singer.

Strange? Maybe. But she was right. She was the best torch singer in a thousand years. Right up there with Billie Holiday and Etta James. Right there with Bessie Smith, Esther Williams and Ella Fitzgerald. Immortals. Goddesses. Their names would be worshipped to the end of time. Their images would be etched in stone. Ruby's name would live on only in the minds of the drunken souls who chanced by the Lonely Hearts Café, a rundown bar by the railroad tracks on the sorry side of Jazztown.

Her distinctive style and phrasing intact, her majestic tone slowly eroding with the glory days of youth when her physical beauty once captured a thousand bills for a single nude sitting.

That perfect body a memory now, she took the stage for another midnight show, her loyal lover at a slightly out-of-tune piano, all that remained of the promise and the dream was a free room above the bar, gratuity drinks from admiring strangers and just enough in tips to get by day to day, night to night. None of that mattered. Nothing mattered but the song. The music never abandoned her. She let it sink into her soul, soothing her mind and easing her haunted memories aside. The piano man knew her as a preacher knows Ecclesiastes.

He followed every gesture and expression, easing her forward like the devoted lover he was.

It was a song she'd sang a thousand times before, maybe more, about a good man gone bad. It was the story of her life. Every song was another chapter and every chapter was a variation on the same theme.

Ruby had always been a sucker for a good looking man with style and a good line. She was always left holding the bag. Good loving and good times. Broken hearts and bad times. Ruby sang the blues. The words were no longer important. The story was as boring as the seventh rerun of a familiar sitcom. It was her lilting voice, her woeful manner and the depth of her performance that made her unforgettable. Every man left a part of himself at the Lonely Hearts Café. Every man in Jazztown was a little in love with its treasured sad eyed lady.

Tonight something was different. You couldn't put your finger on it. The crowd was attentive and respectful but no one suspected anything. The same old bartender served the same old drinks to mostly the same hard drinking customers. The piano man played the same riffs and Ruby sang the same songs.

She took a drink of hard liquor and began the last song of the night still in the dark. As she found the pool of light that revealed the lines of her face, the gentle wrinkles accenting her crow's feet graced with mascara, her voice soared like an eagle on an updraft and dove like a kingfisher to the liquid depths of the universal soul. The muses, the graces and the gods in heaven cried a river in shame. So palpable was the silence when she aced the final note that you could hear a cockroach scurrying beneath the bar the instant she finished.

A tear sprang from her eye and ran down Ruby's cheek. A sacred tear of surrender. A tribute to divine perfection. Every man and every woman in the Lonely Hearts Café knew they would never reach so close to heaven as they were in that sacred moment.

Only the piano man and Ruby truly grasped the meaning in its profundity. Ruby would never sing again. She would drink to her heart's content. The people of Jazztown would take care of her every need. And every night around midnight at the Lonely Hearts Café someone would whisper:

"There she is: the greatest blues singer the world has ever known."

Ruby would smile, accept their kindness, decline every invitation to sing or offer to dance and sit hour after hour in perfect contentment.

MERCHANT OF APHRODITE

The room held a locker room odor of overworked adrenal glands and something more – sweat and something else, something pungent and something sweet.

She was a sweet young thing for the age of thirty-five, crossed between an artist and a pornographic queen of the bump and grind jive.

She had divide eyes: one knowing, one forgiving, one repulsed and one inviting, one teasing and one divine.

She was a dancer on a stage of fire where only ice survives.

Her movement slick and smooth as blue suede shoes revealed her soul and a rose tattoo on the cheek of her sleek and tender side.

She was a vampire of desire feeding frenzy the inertia of her all too willing prey.

"Take me with your mind," she said between pelvic thrusts. "I like it that way."

She turned to let her upper fall and teased her perfect breasts erect. He traced them with the tongue of his imagination.

She was no vampire. She gave more than she received. She was a merchant of Aphrodite. Sweet Eros. Sweet disease.

THE GAMBLER

Drunk again and the irony escaped him. Like a blind man railing against the night, he'd come to the one place that could not ease his pain. Another Jack Daniels and the memory fades. A wise old codger, the barkeep had seen his kind before.

"Say pal, you might want to go easy on it."

The gambler shrugged and downed another.

"Tomorrow's another day."

"Not for me it aint."

His words were a little slurred. Another JD and he would need no words.

"For me there's only yesterday."

"Sounds like a song."

The gambler had lost his sense of humor.

"A week ago I was on top of the world!"

"We've all been there, pal."

"A run of bad luck, a string of snake eyes, a mistaken identity, a simple twist of fate, straight against a flush, flush against a full house, a stacked deck, a hustler with the face of an angel, a sudden turn in the market, short end of the stick and now it's Black Tuesday! I'm sleeping with the cockroaches in the gutter of broken dreams."

He slammed his JD and tapped the bar for another. This time a voice emerged from the other end of the bar.

"You're not the only one down on his luck, pal. Don't wallow in it."

The gambler took a second glance and bit.

"What's your name, buddy?"

"Jack," he said with a wry grin – the only kind he possessed. "And I'm here to deliver a message."

"I'm listening."

Maybe he was and maybe he wasn't.

"It's the only thing my father ever told me that stuck."

"Yeah?"

"Yeah."

They stared each other down like the last players at the table in the dark end of a long night. Jack flipped a silver dollar on the bar, pulled on his black leather coat and headed for the door. He turned back for the message.

"There's no such thing as chance."

They could hear his Harley rev outside as the gambler downed another JD and collapsed face first on the floor.

KID OF COOL & THE NEON SIGN

Platinum blonde of the Marilyn mold
Skirt split to the hilt of a well-shaped hip
Deep brown eyes sleepy time seductive
Lips poised for pleasure

Old enough to be his mother
Smart enough to know better

A contender for the King of Cool
Cigarette dangling from his lower lip
Blue jean jacket skull and crossbones
Live Free or Die!

She crossed her legs in a manner that draws all eyes –
especially his. The pale gray clouds of smoke parted at her
command and drew him in for a closer look. A red neon sign
clicked in the back of his brain: Endangered Cool. Her ruby
red lips formed a circle and the tip of her tongue gently
grazed the edge of her upper teeth.

It moved him like an alto sax in minor key blowing cool
breeze through a steamy night on Bourbon Street. He stood
when his legs allowed and made his move with his hippest
jazzman strut.

A distinguished gentleman in silver gray and two tone
shoes, padded shoulder double breast, emerged from smoke
and shadow to sit beside her with a smile. He signaled the
waiter and she made him with her eyes: Kid of Cool grew
up.

Sweet tease, he thought.

Sweet dreams of jaded kind.

She bestowed a knowing smile and promised him a future on the streets of Jazztown.

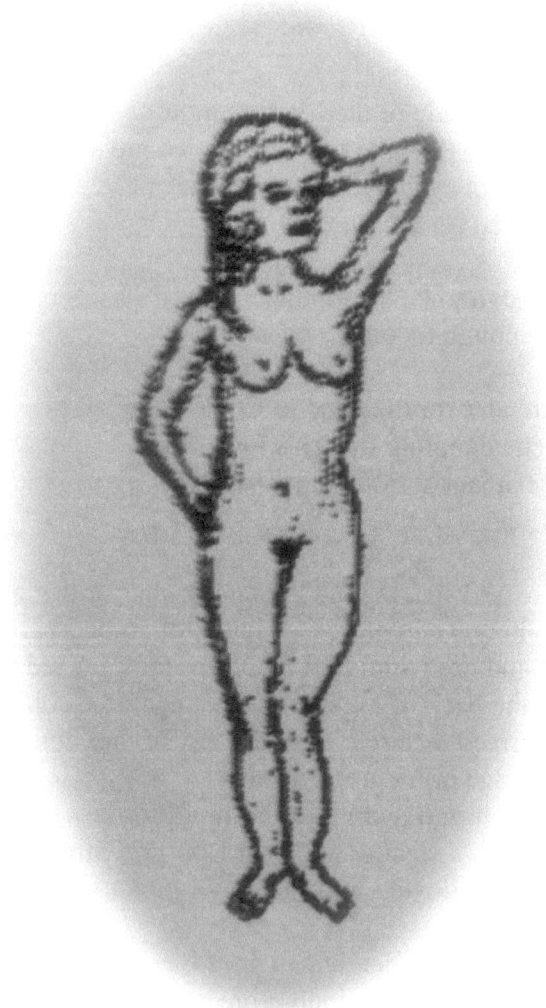

Marilyn Mold

THE TRUMPET PLAYER

For nine years he wandered the barren streets of Jazztown. For nine years he hit the lonely taverns, the Jazztown bars, the darkened corners and forgotten spaces where spirits such as his sought refuge and the company of sympathetic souls. For nine years he tried with all his soul to transform the sound of his battered horn into the deep bone marrow tones of a tenor sax. For nine years he savored that rare glimpse of atonement – those brief and deeply personal moments when everything fit like a tailored suit or a perfect coupling of ecstasy. For nine years he nursed his dream like an adopted love child.

Then one night he awakened in the company of ants on a concrete bed in the back alley of some forgotten nightmare. He heard the sound of music, the music that sprang from the center of his being. He pulled out his battered trumpet, fixed his mouthpiece and blew. He blew from the source of all things though he feared it would steal his life. He blew and he heard the soulful tones he had always heard within his head. He blew and his spirit rose beyond his physical being, beyond the streets of Jazztown, beyond the smell and drudgery of back alleyways, to grasp the very pinnacle of existence. He touched his god.

He had reached the crucible of his journey through life. He blew knowing that everything hereafter would only be redundant. He blew until he could blow no more.

He collapsed against a brick wall and slid to the concrete below. Exhausted, he removed his mouthpiece, replaced his horn in its tattered shell and shed a tear of joy.

FEED THE MONKEY

She was a streamline model nobody's whore
Breasts the size of golden delicious apples
She pressed the cheeks of her veneer
Against the mirrored image of her own reflection
And twisted her ripened nipples to a state of elation

She mouthed the words twenty bucks
As if licking a lemon lollipop
Twenty bucks to feel the force of her machine
Finely tuned and oiled to perfection

Shake it baby bend it to the rod and core
Squeeze and squirm on the polished floor
Drive it like a locomotive full of steam
Atomic powered submarine
Quake and make it moan
Devour liquid lust

Glide the stream of wanton dreams
Buck it like a wild stallion
Ride the mile high roller coaster
Take it down and ride again

Take me to the poorhouse
Relieve me of my senses
Drop me off the edge of sanity
Lay me down in Tupelo honey
Leave me on the sea of floating fantasy

RANDOM JACK

You've got to feed the monkey she whispered
Beyond the flame of gone and far away

Don't worry I replied
The monkey has been fed

THE REMINGTON

The world thought him crazy but harmless. Some even thought him capable of occasional genius. So in his old age he was allowed certain eccentricities.

He sat before his Remington for hours without moving, without thinking, without feeling, until the world around him became darkness, total darkness, and his mind became a clean blank palate. He began his mantra:

Free yourself of words…they have no meaning
Free yourself of history…it is not real
Free yourself of senses…it is perception
Free yourself of perception…it is distortion

Before long the words began to form themselves, telling the story of his enchanted life: a maze of wonders beyond imaging. One is the number of the life force. Two is the number of opposites. Three is the number of philosophy. Four is the number of space and time. Five is the number of eternal war. Six is the number of unity. Seven is the number of alternate reality. Eight is the number of infinity. Nine is the number divine.

He read what had written in his absence. A smile wrinkled the lines of his face. "No one will understand," he gloated.

A poisonous thought gripped his turgid brain like a vice. The typewriter is its own device! It has its own agenda, its own history and preconceptions! All he had written over all these years his typewriter had altered every intention! This was not his creation! There would be no creation!

RANDOM JACK

With the strength of a younger man he hoisted the old Remington from its wooden perch and dropped it without a second thought out the third story window. He watched with childlike glee as it crashed to the pavement below, bent and shattered beyond repair.

He grabbed a pen and placed a clean white sheet of paper before him. He began the process anew.

The Remington

ESMERALDA

Esmeralda on the streets of Jazztown
Spinning with the core of creation
Eyes dancing fire rage desire
Soul tempting ecstasy

Ancient peyote winds howl and roar
Beyond words beyond passion
Beyond the edge of all reason

A body as an instrument of faith
Finely tuned to raise the rod the dwells within
The secret soul of self

Blast the fuel of pure devotion
Untouched by the hand of social righteousness
Cast out the wagging tongues and bulging eyes
Of those who cannot walk the streets
Naked and alone

You are the wind the blessed child
The chosen of the nameless flock
They follow their noses through the maze
While you rise to greet the dawn

You are the object of desire
The masses dream of you
And pray to meet you in another life

Dance and let the masses dream

RANDOM JACK

Sweet nectar of life
Sweet moment of perfection
Yours to embrace
Ours to behold

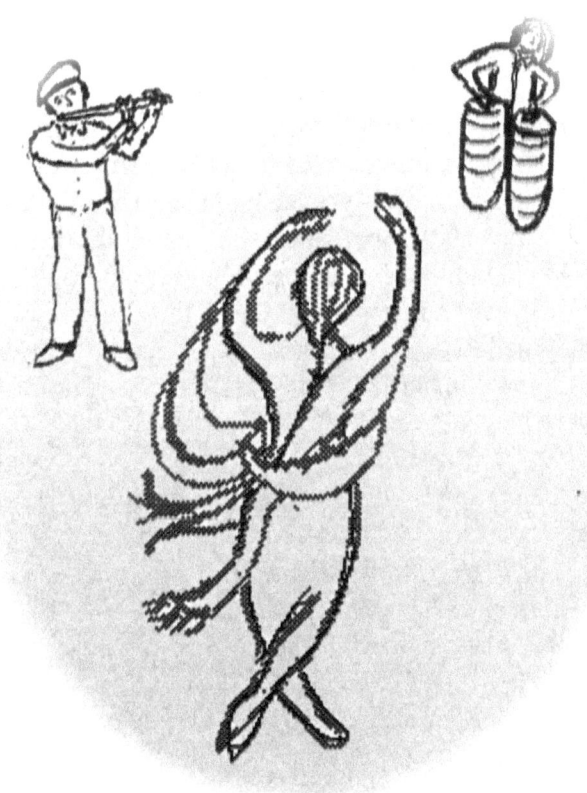

Esmeralda on the streets of Jazztown

HALLOWED CROSSING

He was a jazzman poet living in clouds of smoke, blinded to the ways of the working world. Welcomed in every jazz joint in Jazztown, he was given the stage to fill the gap between sets. The musicians always left the backstage door ajar and tuned one ear to the man on the mike, hungry for his words and intonations as they smoked their worries into oblivion. He was the only man in Jazztown they bought a drink. His low and raspy voice summoned the image of a bullfrog, like a man who liked his JD a little too much for far too long. He held an honored place in the court of Jazztown bars. They called him Ray for no other reason than he was blind as a newborn kitten. He was more a Charlie Parker man, himself.

I see you dancing naked under blue moonlight
I hear thundering rain and stars in flight
I see your perfect body unleashed
In dreams of passion and raw desire
I see your hunger filled in rhapsodies
Crying more and come again
I see your tender body open like a broken dam
And rushing whitewater crash and burn
In waves of pulsing grace
I see your love lust and tender mercy
Spring from your root and center core
The raging fire of sweet Eros
Radiating in sultry light
Awakening from a thousand year sleep
To taste the dawn

RANDOM JACK

You and I are lovers from a million lives
Before this hallowed crossing
I greet you with a gentle kiss
And praise your solemn beauty

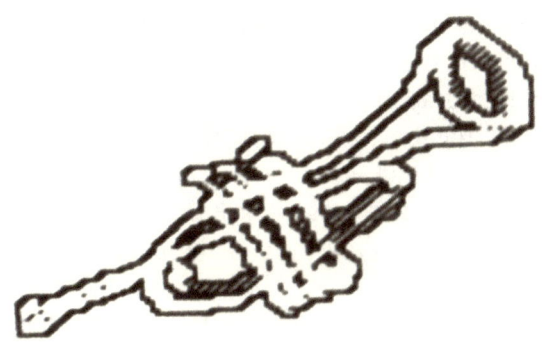

THE SERPENT'S TRAIL

It was not the gentle sway of music that guided her motion like the overflow of expensive champaign. She glided through the crowd of immobile bodies in black and gray and captured his wondering eye.

It was not the naked line of her silken hips, the fullness of her ruby lips nor the grace with which she slipped into her evening wrap of gray and silver fox.

It was not the brazen outline of her full white breasts beneath the sheer black satin of her blouse. It was not the soft gentle wave of her long dark hair or the deep pools of sorrow within her brooding eyes or the pure Picasso lines of her angelic face.

It was the sliver of a glance she left behind that left him stunned, gasping for life in a lifeless room. He followed her across the banquet floor, across the plush furnishings of the hotel lobby to the golden arch of the elevator door. He watched the moving arrow to its stop at number seven, pointing the way to lover's heaven like Cupid with his bow.

He moved in to meet his longing and saw the promise of destiny in the form of a card on the elevator floor. It read: Seven zero four. His knees buckled as he rose to hold himself in check. He walked the crimson carpet hallway until he found himself before the number of delivery. His breath quickened as he steadied for the close.

He did not knock but entered like a ghost in hallowed silence. She felt his presence. In the lighting of the moon through an open window she let her silken garment flutter softly to the floor, leaving only her high-heeled shoes, black silk stockings and sleek lace panties between his sight and imagination. Moving to a rhythm all her own, her hands swept downward, her thumbs catching the elastic waistband, she lingered before turning and lowering them to her ankles and stepping to the floor.

She stood in full glory and met his eyes of fire with her own. Brushing back her hair to offer up a better view, she traced the longing of his eyes with her fingers. She moved like a floating drift of smoke to sit upon her velvet bedside and opened like the petals of a rose in bloom.

He stood before the goddess of his devotion and placed himself at her mercy, parting her moistened lips with his. Like a serpent in sand her body writhed as if in agony to the rhythm of their collective heartbeat. He let go and made his sacred offering to close the last divide.

No more would love be mystery, no longer passion veiled. He tasted the fruit of the lover's tree and traced the serpent's trail.

KARMA COMEDIA

"Karma Comedia!" the poet laughed with disdain. It was his description of a shrinking circle within society: the art of the inane.

Jack turned to the bar and let the poet's grating voice dwindle into white noise.

"What's the matter?" she said in a soulful tone, three stools down at the bar. The voice belonged to a beautiful woman still in her sentient prime, appealing to a man of depth who often entertained himself with rhyme.

"Don't you like poetry?" she asked when she caught his eye.

"I love poetry," he replied. He carried Yeats in his pocket and read Neruda when opportunity allowed. "I came here for the jazz."

"He sucks," she said with a gesture to the stage.

He smiled and asked her name.

"Ruby," she smiled in reflection. They shared the art of reading minds. Jack was an amateur to her mastery. "I came here with him." Once again she gestured to the stage and the poet still milking his time.

"Yeah," she said. "I don't know what I was thinking." She probed him for a moment and seemed to savor what she tasted with her rose petal lips. "Like to give him a rise?"

"Why not?" he shrugged. He needed one and he wasn't the kind to back away from a fight.

She ambled to the adjacent barstool while Jack admired the movement of a woman who knew how to talk with her hips. The rhythm of jazz thrived in her bloodline. She let the softness of her thigh graze the firmness of his to test the balance of chemistry.

"Hmm," she purred in sweet affirmation.

"Another jack and coke," he said.

She didn't wonder how or why he knew. It went without saying. They spoke of WC Handy, Ellington and James, Charley Parker, Monk and Coltrane. She sang a sultry blues into his ear. He almost melted and wondered at the mysteries of life. He didn't notice that the poet's voice had faded along with the poet's light. A rustling in the bar behind him made him turn in time to catch the poet's clutched fists and lower him to the bar with a thud. A knife dropped to the wooden floor, jack and coke scattered, and the poet guided to the door.

"Karma Comedia!" Ruby smiled.

The poet spent the night alone.

Jack took his place in Ruby's feather bed and garden of delights.

BLACK LEOTARDS

An angel in black leotards beneath ragged blue jeans, openings placed to charge erotic dreams, she was a child of the sixties and a woman out of time.

Free will, free love, free mind...

She wants it so badly she can smell it as she walks into the hipster jazz café looking for the lucky man to spread her wings and take her for a ride. She sets her sight and marks him twice with her wanting eyes.

Free will, free love, free mind...

She takes a corner seat, unties her knotted blouse and orders up a cappuccino on ice. A man of certain experience about her age, give or take another life, in work shirt, dungarees and frazzled blackish hair, turns to scope her scene and measure her intent. He hasn't seen this action in a while.

She rolls and lights a cigarette, inviting him to undress her with her Greta Garbo eyes. He finds it easy to comply and suffers no resistance.

Free will, free love, free mind...

He strolls to her table and dredges up a weary line: Do I know you?

"Not by name," she smiles and offers him a waiting seat with her shapely leg.

He sits in silent contemplation of the gods of fortune, a

vision of her naked beauty dancing in his brain.

"Woodstock," he says – not knowing why.

"Woodstock," she replies and drinks to praise the moment in reflection. They've made a connection in record time.

Free will, free love, free mind...

He follows her to exaltation where fantasies remove all former life, discarding fool's disguises if only for the night.

Free will, free love, free mind...

She leaves him with moon shadows in his eyes, retracing naked memories reflected in a pool of shining innocence – no guilt, no possession, no remorse.

Free will, free love, free mind...

BULLDOG ROMANCE

"Women are all the same," he barks with a side angle glare at the brunette beauty down the line. "Kill 'em all before they kill you!"

She doesn't look up, seeming absorbed in particles of fluttering light drifting through the amber vision of scotch on the rocks. She's heard it all before.

"What's a dame like you doing in a dump like this?" Loud and more obnoxious than the screech of a second grade chalkboard.

She closes her eyes to prepare for the jolt: another sad confrontation with a beer bellied dolt whose idea of romance is a dropkick to the chest, one oiled paw scratching his scrotum, the other swiping drool from three days growth.

"You're right, Mac." She speaks in a voice between a growl and a whisper. "I'm too damned good looking to deal with pigs like you."

"I'm no pig!" he roars with a jowl and belly roll. "I'm a goddamned bulldog!"

Planted between antagonists, Jack rises by instinct as the bulldog makes his move. He hears a voice he recognizes as his own say: "Leave her alone."

Bulldog stays his panting breath of stale cigars and rye whiskey with a wry grin that says: Must be my lucky day! He makes the move he learned from Brando in *A Streetcar Named Desire* when he slaps Stella into submission: Right head fake, pounce and drive it home.

Jack watches him like a passenger on a train watches a bobbing power line, stunned by its predictability. His head throbs as Bulldog lowers it to the bar three times: whap,

whap, whap! He lets the throbbing subside before he stands against his will and staggers to steady, hold and brace.

Bulldog's grin spreads to cackling glee as he's shouldered to the door by two barmen the size of gorillas.

"Better than sex!" he cackles as they cast him to the sea of city lights outside. "Better than sex!"

"You want to press charges, Mac?"

"Fuck it. Give me a drink."

"Put it on my tab," she purrs and cozies up beside him to dress his wounded manhood.

"Slick move, Mac," she says as she positions his knee between her thighs and squeezes away the pain. She wipes the blood from his brow with an old bar rag. He feels the tips of her pointed breasts brush against his forearm and moans.

"More balls than brains," she mutters. "I like that in a man."

"Whatever turns you on," he says as he buries his head in the bosom of barroom paradise.

Whatever turns you on.

FLOWER IN THE RAIN

Trembling with desire
Thirst running through my veins
I dove into her scarlet web
Tasting her sweet nectar
Passion like a river flowing
Cresting white water rush and quiver
Like a flower in the rain

She pulled my lips to hers, sweeping the dew that still
held there, alive and fresh like tangerine pie, a vacuum filled
with yearning, driving, throbbing, swirling, writhing, twisting
like a snake in clover, a field of wildflowers in a hurricane
wind. She pulled me in and out again, casting self aside, her
lava flowing in endless waves of madness, joy and love of
Mother Nature's sacred womb. Like a flower in the rain.

POOLSIDE VIEW

You could tell by the way she moved her hips she was experienced despite her youth. She dressed with a hint of sixties style, hair pulled back under a red bandana, her blooming breasts beneath a loose white cotton blouse, jeans faded to fashion. Her dark mascara, blush and ruby red lipstick broke the pattern but served its own purpose, drawing focus to her bedroom eyes – an invitation to delight or a tease to incite the fantasy of a weary stranger who chanced upon a poolside view.

I was sitting on the balcony above the pool when she flashed her finest come-and-get-it cool. She appeared under moonlight for a midnight swim. I held my breath and took it in as she let the robe about her shoulders fall to a poolside chair and dove into the water beneath my midnight stare.

Not an ounce of excess upon her sleek young form, she appealed to my desire like a shelter in the storm. Toweling her body dry she glanced up in my direction and settled in repose. Her back arched to unfasten the upper of her cover, her hands assumed the nature of an overseeing lover.

Her eyes found mine and closed, her legs spread wide, she yielded to her hunger and heard the pounding of my heart. "Dear God!" I screamed a muffled cry and melted to the floor where I remained until my body found its core. When I awakened she was nowhere to be found though the waters, still in motion, scattered moonlight all around.

EXECUTIVE ALLURE

Her allure was the executive kind. She possessed a powerful presence, illuminating eyes and a passion sheltered carefully in words. She'd worked most of her life to hide the beatific blessings of her birth yet even the unimaginative lines of her attire could not disguise her sensual design.

Her voice was eminently sincere, full and in the lower part of her natural register. She caught his eye in the midst of a tired crowd whom she addressed with professional concern. She was drawn. His eyes alone were alive. His alone held the fire she had buried within.

She bowed with grace and bid him follow. He yielded to the magnet of her desire, untapped, unspoiled. When he drew close enough to touch, she whispered:

Do powerful women turn you on?

Always, he replied.

She offered him her hand and in it a key.

Tonight at nine, she whispered.

Her voice was not her own. It belonged to the woman she had longed to be and the woman he longed to meet.

Time stood immobile for hours until at last she welcomed him at her hotel door. She let her silken robe fall gently from her shoulders.

For his eyes only she reserved this sacred sight. For his eyes only held the liberating light. A form infinitely too exquisite for words yet his eyes held to hers and breathed the essence of desire, hot and pure and innocent.

Without thought or conscious movement they came together and danced the dance of sweet amour, lost in texture, flesh and scent, lost in harmonies of pleasure. They would dance forever more.

Do you like powerful men? he smiled.

Always, she replied.

MOTHER OF PEARL

A place of infinite beauty, pure and pristine, it reminded him of childhood dreams, walking through fields of endless flowers, swimming in streams of translucent waters, soaring with the wind over tree tops in blue moonlight.

He wandered without care and could not recall how he came to stand before her. Lost among towering sunflowers, so brightly colored against the backdrop of a blue velvet sky, something called to him in crimson and sang to him in gold.

He followed as a child follows the player of heartstring melodies until he came to the secret garden where she, reclining on a bed of white rose petals, awakened with a start.

He lingered on the curl and wave of her dark and henna hair until it swept over him, comforting his soul with warmth and soothing. Her eyes were enchanted in an amber hue, her lips a natural ruby, her skin a delicate mother of pearl, her soft round breasts perfectly contoured, the work of a master artist or a generous god.

Awakening before him, sensing her lover's gaze, her nipples erect and wanting eyes, she beckoned him come embrace her delight.

He came to her and she gathered him in, breathed and caressed him, folded him in, pulled and gripped, swallowed him in. She purified him in a baptism of erotic love.

Sweet angel of no tomorrow
Sweet ecstasy of ending sorrow
Sweet dream of ever always ever more…

MORE TALES FROM JAZZTOWN

RANDOM JACK

Decked in Johnny B Good patent leather soles, double breast and padded shoulder zoot suit, gangster to the core, he turned the corner and strutted to the beat down a cobblestone alleyway at dusk.

Inside the Paradise Bar a cat in tan loafers, cool and wrinkle free despite beads of sweat on his pale and lifeless brow, eyed the unattended redhead once or twice too much.

He couldn't help but notice
As he scanned the local clime
There was murder in the air that night
There was murder in his mind

"What's shakin' Red?" he said and ordered up a brew. She gave a glance, that's all it took; he gave the cat a second look. He looked away a fraction of a moment too late.

There was murder in the air that night
And murder was his fate

She lifted her glass to toast: "Here's to you, stranger! As long as you're here, you might as well put down a few."

He drank his last and left the bar but he never made it to his car. Random Jack followed to explain:

There's murder in the air tonight
And murder is my game

Imprisoned by the corners of his life, the warden allowed

him three hours a day to write or masturbate or pray. He sat at his Remington, let his mind drift on seven winds, and waited for a golden opportunity – or maybe it was gray. In the midst of his darkness the sun shined for just a little longer than his whiskey warmed his soul. He took it as a sign and started to unwind the layers over time that sheltered him from harm.

Let the thunder roar he cried. Let the lightning strike! No act of god or nature will keep me from this flight!

And so he wrote. Like a crazed madman, like an inspired muse, like Moses with the word of god still ringing in his ears, like an Einstein flash of insight, like Ludwig at his keyboard, like Shakespeare in his prime, he wrote. The words spilled forth like a river of passion. He scarcely had time to retrieve them. On and on they came and came, thunder cracking like the whip of Apollo, its electric charm wrapping him like a leather glove, like a liquid lover's embrace. On and on until the words became letters and the letters became symbols streaming across the page in paths of their own choosing. On and on as if he'd never known how to write until now. On and on and on and on until they came crashing to a halt of their own volition with an implosion and a ball of flame that blinded him to his soul and marrow.

There he sat motionless and dumb until his body finally returned to its home.

It was then that he killed the mother and her offspring for their innocence and faith. He cut them up for dog food but the dogs would not partake. And so he feasted on the product of his grizzly deed and hung their heads on flagpoles for everyone to see.

He did not utter a word – not a syllable or sound – to rally his defense until they strapped him to the chair and read his last rites.

"Wait!" he cried. "Please!" he implored. "Give me one

last try!"

> Too late, my friend, though it is a crime
> Art requires both inspiration and time

In a world as soft as butterflies, as violent as a raging sea, there's no such thing as random chance.

"Do you believe?" the preacher demanded.
"Believe in what?" Jack replied.
"Do you believe in the power of the Lord?"
"Sure, why not?"

The Jack is back with a tale to tell of politicians giving flaccid speeches, words drooling into the crowd, dissipating in the pallid atmosphere. The Jack is back with a tale to tell of singers with nothing more than Jesus on their minds or in their hearts despite their best intentions. The Jack is back with a tale to tell of fireworks over dark waters, bursting in palpable tear drops, sending higher minds into acid dreams and wagging the tongues of doddlers, of tired songs and tired symphonies, dedicating art to the uninspired, of people packed so close together they are forced to deal with each other as something more than vague entities, holders of space.

Little do they suspect that Jack wanders among them, infiltrating their collective consciousness, tapping their energies like a well taps water. Winding his way like a silent serpent to the center of their gathering, the solar plexus of their collective being, only the most observant notice his presence. The crowd lets him pass like a beggar at the door of a restaurant. He does not exist.

He lets out his line and watches it bob and weave like a jig at high tide. He waits for the moment and strikes like whiplash in a rear end collision.

"Viva Che!" he cries and vanishes into the black hole of

the night.
"Something to think about," he whispers.
Another Fourth of July.

Gone like a distant memory. Gone like the mists of the northern Pacific. Only two revolutions removed yet as distant as a Tibetan monk atop a Himalayan peak. As remote as peace of mind or gently falling snow or eyes without doubt or love without claim.

Gone, gone, gone. Systemic instability, paralysis, imbalance, schizo scherzo, a dance of fools around a pagan queen. Squatting in the brambles of his charred and beaten body, he could not lift an arm to swat away the flies. Devoured by the beasts of prey. Purpose, meaning and harmony destroyed in the blink of a battered eye.

Awakening from an incubus, beads of liquid fear dripping from his brow, straining his stilted view, he caught a glimpse of reality beyond the senses. He would never be the same.

His mother often said: If you have nothing good to say, don't say anything at all. He did not speak for years.

BLUE VELVET IN THE CITY OF JAZZ

I fell in love at first sight, at first smell, at first sound, taste and touch. She was the first woman I encountered who was not beyond reproach, the first to welcome my embrace, and the first to cradle me in her dreams through the lustful nights of my youth. As I listened to her heartbeat, as I watched her parade, as I moved between her shadows, I came to understand her timeless beauty, her eternal allure. I came to recognize her voice, soft and sultry, as a song of the sirens and a tribute to a million souls' sacrifice.

I answered her call and crossed the threshold for a first taste of sin. She whispered in my ear, a voice without words, as sweet as harmony – enchanting, disturbing, sophisticated yet raw like a fine jazz. She injected my loins with insatiable desire. I knew then I would do anything for her.

I walked the streets of the jazz district, wandering in and out of bars, trailing strippers, shadowing pimps, hanging with hustlers, listening for that sultry voice and the woman who possessed it. I felt her presence everywhere. It was in the mist that flowed from the ancient cemetery where the Voodoo Queen lay waiting. It traveled through the dark alleys and down the avenues across bridges and byways to the swamplands and the sea. I felt it in the viscous darkness where ancient stone formed ancient walls, shrouded in moss and vine, standing the millennia, defying time itself. I saw her face in every crowd, around every corner of every street and alleyway. I heard her laughter, like a desert mirage, always beyond my reach, teasing me with grace and style like a lady of old time burlesque. I serenaded her under street lamps, hoping to entice her with the ghosts of jazz greats.

I was a wide-eyed fool in love with mystery, enchanted by her dark secret and unspoken promise. I took an apartment on the outskirts of town, where nobody asked what my dreams were made of and nobody cared if I played my sax until the vampires were tucked in their coffins. I was alone with my dreams, my desires, my disease. I took some stand-in gigs, played for tips on the street, and made enough to get by while I continued the search.

Life struggled on for months, maybe years, without noticeable change. The relativity of time is this town's creed. I met a man whose story was he took a wrong turn off the expressway and woke up thirty years later in Beggar's Alley. Time is measured by the mirror – which is why there are so few here, except in the darkness of bars, the cathedrals of forgotten dreams.

The time came when I turned up the lights and took a good look. I felt cheated. I felt like a man who traded the best of his life for a cheap bottle of red wine. I was caught in a rut, feeling the strain, my dreams fading like a tattered postcard, like a rotting corpse in a Louisiana swamp.

It was then that she came to me. On a desperate moonlit night, on the balcony of my favorite dive, I was breathing in the cool jazz when I looked down on the parade of saints and sinners, across a swarm of human madness, and I saw her face. She was a spirit of raw beauty, dark eyes and blonde skin, her delicate lines forming a portrait of innocence belying the knowledge and wisdom of her eyes. She grabbed me hard in a place without words, a place so pure I could not have imagined it before that moment.

I dove into the crowd and hunted her down like a junkie in search of a fix. When I asked who she was, she replied, "Blue Velvet." It was the only name I ever knew her by. If she had another, I never knew it, never heard it whispered in passing, and never saw it written down on a chance piece of paper. I never asked her what she did or where she came from. It was understood. She would always be a mystery. She would always be Blue Velvet.

She didn't have a job in the usual sense because she was always free. She inhabited the cafes by day and the taverns by night. She was not a prostitute or a stripper though she could have gathered treasures by either profession. What was she? It was not an easy question. She was a woman and an enigma. She was as unreachable as the most distant star yet she belonged to the city of jazz and the city held her as a mother holds a favored child.

I became her slave. Everything was Blue Velvet. I breathed, ate, drank and dreamed Blue Velvet. I played Blue Velvet on my tenor sax for hours on end without pause. I reached tones that reverberated in my soul, notes and nuances I could never touch before. Everything I cherished dwelled in her eyes. Everything I valued was in her grace. Everything I treasured was in her smile. She put my world in balance. She was my queen and my universe and I surrendered all my love, my will, and my soul. My devotion and passion were so pure it radiated to the very heart of the city where it was received by her underworld Queen.

I had always thought it was a legend, like Robert Johnson at the crossroads but when she spoke to me with clear intent and distinct words, I understood that she was real. She was unhappy. She was jealous. A love like mine for Blue Velvet could not belong to anyone but her.

"Come baby," she said. "It is me you want."

Sitting at a balcony table, sipping wine, Blue Velvet sensed my distraction.

"What is it?" she asked.

"Nothing," I replied.

"Don't you dare!" said the Queen. "You turn your back on me now, there be no second chance!"

Her voice held a thick Caribbean accent, summoning visions of voodoo and dark arts. It rumbled with raw power like an earthquake of the soul.

"I've got to go," I mumbled.

Blue Velvet placed her hand on mine and nuzzled closer. "No, you don't," she whispered. Her breast on my forearm, waves of desire channeled through my spine, culminating in a full-body tremor, a tingling in my fingers and a glaze on my vision, painting everything before me in translucent green light. I felt life itself surging through me and realized how dead, how imprisoned, how desperate I had become.

Who is this woman? What powers does she command? What master does she serve? She had filled my hopes with the promise of a child while injecting my desire with an addiction stronger than morphine. I wanted her more than I wanted life, more than a hound with an itch for a bitch in heat, even more than the dream of the underground Queen.

The Queen laughed inside my skull and sunk her claws more deeply. It was as if she was hardwired into my brain. Whatever Blue Velvet promised, the Queen would offer more. If I could win her blessing, there was no limit to what I could accomplish and who I could become. I could play like Sidney Benet or Charlie Parker with a twist. She held the promise before me like a golden chalice of sweet sweat fantasy. She was the disease and I was her playground.

There was but one thing the Queen could not offer; the one thing that trumped all else in my aching heart: the love of Blue Velvet.

I was caught in the crossfire, trapped between the yearning of my heart and the desire of my eternal soul. I could neither advance nor retreat. Surrounded by traps and temptations, I could not move for fear of falling and, if I fell, I feared it would be a decline without end, a never-ending pit of sorrow and despair.

Blue Velvet comforted me with a gentle smile. She took me by the arm and together we walked down the street where painted people, in joy and revelry, parted as if to reveal our path. We walked into a darkened alley, where we were alone in the shadows of a timeless city, alone with the beating of a million hearts, and alone with the rhythm of eternal jazz.

It was a place somehow familiar as if I had walked this path before. I recognized its chiseled walls, overrun with creeping vines. I sensed its hidden enclaves where the eyes of dark spirits glowed like those of an owl in an ancient forest. I knew where we were going for, in the early stages of my disease, I had peered through these same windows and knocked on these same doors but none opened to my pleas. We were approaching the underground, wherein the Queen was waiting in her lair.

It was a dead end, surrounded by tall brick buildings, dark and dank, air so thick you drank it into your lungs. Suddenly, where nothing was before, there appeared a passage where we descending a spiral staircase to a great expanse below. The floor and ceiling were made of stone, supported by great stone columns, but there were no walls. It was a space so vast I could see no end. A thin veil of mist clung to the floor and an eerie green illumination seemed to emanate from the stone itself.

It was a world within a world, sheltered from the sun, hidden from the overlords and common dregs of the city. It stole my breath to think that something so vast and ancient could exist undetected, beyond reach and exposure. How and when it came to be seemed to me as unanswerable as the origins of humanity.

Blue Velvet pulled me close, her leg against my thigh, her breasts against my chest, her lips a whisper from my own. She steadied and strengthened my resolve with a charge of electro-erotic visions.

At the edge of my consciousness, I could hear the sounds of human activity – music, dance, conversation and carnality. I saw a bearded man, his face aglow, emerging from the mist. He seemed to spring from the floor, as if the underworld gave way to an underworld below. I saw others emerge, both men and women, faces painted in strange expressions of intense desire, fear, hope and desperation. I imagined an endless maze of tunnels and passages connecting chambers of stone, cities of darkness, palaces of gold.

A parade of people emerged from the mist only to slip away into the subterranean corridors of stone. They were alive with the rhythm of jazz but they lacked its soul. It seemed they had left the world behind, lost their names and faces, and the rhythm they now stepped to was alive but it was not their own. Not one of them made a move toward the stairway to freedom. No one tried to escape.

Had they lost their way or had they only lost hope? Had they sold their souls to the underworld Queen? Would I face the same choice? Was there a choice?

The sound of the Queen's laughter reached out to us and swallowed all else. We moved toward her, descending a passageway, weaving through a maze of corridors without hesitation or doubt, as if the map was implanted in our brains, until we came to the very heart of the underworld: the chamber of the Queen.

She was an exceptionally tall Caribbean woman, thin but strong, with bronze skin and dark piercing eyes that glowed with same green illumination that pervaded her kingdom of stone. She was a vision of power and eternal knowledge, sitting on a throne of fur, surrounded by wall hangings with spiritual symbols and mystic designs, hair dancing like Medusa's serpents, her laughter reverberating in glimmering candlelight. At her side was a book of spells and potions. Before her was a circle of sacred objects, the wing of an owl, plants and pendulums, with a cauldron at its core. She waved her hand and we sat before her, clinging to each other for strength.

"Welcome to my sanctuary," she intoned.

"Who are you?" I asked when my tongue found voice.

"I am the master of all you see. I am the heartbeat of jazz. Without its Queen this place would be a swamp for the fishes and the rats. I am more than you can imagine or understand yet I am a woman. Is that what you wanted to know?"

I shook my head though it seemed impertinent and dangerous yet she nodded with approval as she mixed potions, cast spells, and spoke in strange tongues to unseen spirits.

"Why have you summoned us?" I asked.

"Desire," she answered and a wave of pleasure coursed through my body, caressing, soothing, and pleading for surrender. "There be millions here just like you and they all come for the same reason: Desire."

She read my mind as I would read a book, so that I never had to speak aloud. I only had to wonder and she would answer.

"No one here is a prisoner," she explained. "Everyone be free. Free to come, free to go. There is but one rule: If you leave, you cannot return."

I wondered if anyone had ever tried to leave. Was it even possible to turn one's back on the temptations she held before them? The Queen smiled but did not answer.

"I offer you a choice," she said. "It is a simple one: This woman offers you her love. You want love, don't you, pilgrim? You want this woman? I give her to you. Give me the word and she is yours forever and always."

I cannot describe the terror that gripped my heart and shook my world as she spoke these words.

How could I not have known? How could I not have suspected? Blue Velvet was a creature of the underworld. She belonged to the Queen.

I looked into her eyes and I still believed. Her love was true and real, as real as a garden in Paradise. She was the woman of my dreams. She was the heart of my desire. Despite the wrenching of my conscious mind, my heart still opened to Blue Velvet.

"I offer you this and all you desire," said the Queen. "It is all at your command: Music, dance, fantasies, pleasures of the mind and the flesh, adventure, joy and sorrow.

Everything you need to feel alive."

Her words conjured visions so that I saw what she spoke of as real and palpable as stone, as if they were plucked from the depths of my soul. It was a feast of enchantment.

"Shall you turn your back on love, pilgrim? Shall you walk away from all your dreams? The choice be yours and yours alone."

I sensed something wrong, an uncertainty, a discontinuity in the chain of events, a hidden force, like a sudden darkness or the emergence of forgotten shame. It sobered me and allowed me to clear my mind if only for a moment.

Evil. The word slipped into my thoughts without warning. I was not the kind of person to judge. I did not believe in such a construct. The Queen laughed, shaking the walls and echoing through the maze of corridors.

"How old are you?" she demanded. "Old enough to know better, I think. There is no such thing as evil. It is a monster the powers create to explain things to small children. It is the only explanation a child can understand. If you kill a man's child and he kills you in return, is that evil?"

"If I kill a man's child, the evil is within," I replied.

"Not if that child was going to kill yours."

My thoughts stopped mid process and I wondered why this discussion was necessary. I understood why I had been summoned but I could not understand why the all-powerful Voodoo Queen of the underworld would need to persuade me of this or anything else. Why not simply imprint my mind with her beliefs? Why pretend that what I thought mattered to her?

"What you consider evil," she continued, "is only vengeance. There is always a reason a man does wrong. Sometimes it is clear. Sometimes it is hidden. But it is always there, lurking beneath the surface of things."

"Evil is the harm that is done to the innocent," I replied. I did not know why but I felt the necessity to engage her even though my native beliefs were not so distant from hers. I sensed that there was more at stake than intellectual pursuit.

"Ah!" she replied. "So you want me to believe that a hurricane is evil! Earthquakes, disease and floods are evil! So the root of all this evil is the great mother earth!"

She had led me on a circuitous route of thought, trapping me in the web of my own logic. If evil did not exist then I had nothing to fear. I thought back to a time and place when I was certain that evil existed. It was a strange remembrance of a seemingly unremarkable event.

"I knew a couple," I explained. "Both were friends of mine. The woman was an actress, an artist – a truly wonderful person. Her partner was a computer genius and a great guy. I looked to them for advice. I confided in them when I was down."

The Queen nodded with impatience as if she already knew my story. Candlelight danced on the walls and Blue Velvet held tight to my side.

"One night they had a fight. I don't even remember what it was about. It went back and forth, escalating with each pass, until it erupted in violence. My good friend beat her badly. He called me and we took her to the emergency room. Sitting in the hospital, I asked him why he had done it. He replied with one word, as if it explained everything, as if any man would understand. Women, he said. That was all: Women."

The Queen smiled with apparent compassion. "Yes," she sighed. "There are connections that tie us together and tear us apart. Women against men. Men against women. So, though we are all one great circle, there will always be a price to pay for us and for them. It is an ancient grudge. It is shameful. Still, it is only vengeance, my child, though it reaches from beyond the grave. It is not evil."

"You misunderstand," I said. "It was not what he did. It was what he said. It was not the harm. It was the look in his eyes. It was the assumption that I understood."

She shook her head slowly, incanting a spell and drinking

some elixir. She looked into my eyes until I felt her inside of me.

"There is no evil here."

I looked into Blue Velvet's eyes and what I saw, if only for an instant, consumed me and altered my destiny. Beneath the surface of her kindness and affection, I saw a brutal truth. I saw evil. I saw the lie of the underground and its Queen.

I walked out. I returned to the streets a lost and lonely man, a man who had tasted eternal love and walked away, a man who had glimpsed the essence of desire and turned his back forever.

For a very long time I never looked back. Then, one lost summer's night, I felt the need to test my sanity and my resolve. I went back and walked the familiar streets until I found the alley where once I was guided by my love to the underground world of the Voodoo Queen. I stood on the solid ground where once a stairwell had been. I went back to the jazz clubs, taverns, cafes and shops where Blue Velvet and I had been together. I was flooded with memories of her enchanting voice, her exquisite body and perfect porcelain face, but there was nothing more than memories. She was gone. A phantom born of too many nights on the barren streets, on the tear-stained sheets, on the broken dreams of the city of jazz.

I came to understand that it was Blue Velvet who saved me from my own desires and wrestled me away from the clutches of the underground Queen. In a moment of empathy, in the spirit of love, she lifted the veil of beautiful deception just long enough for me to see.

A little sadder and wiser, I went on with my life until one day I found myself in familiar place. I was standing in a courtyard below my favorite café balcony when I heard her whisper from behind me: "There is always a choice." I turned and saw her pure white face, framed by the same dark hair, the same inviting lips, and her enchanting eyes of sorrow and illumination. At once, I felt the pull that had always been beyond my will to resist.

She was only a doll – a porcelain figurine adorning a shop window. I gazed at her for what seemed eternity, trying to comprehend, trying to accept what I could not grasp. Was this the price she paid for my soul? Was this the Queen's revenge?

I could not bear the thought of purchasing her. Hers was a spirit that could never be possessed – not even by the Queen. Yet the thought of leaving her here, trapped in the body of a doll, still caught in the Queen's lair and forced to observe the life she once lived so that I might go free, was even more unbearable.

I laid down my money and took her home. I placed her on the mantel of my fireplace and there she sits to this day. She sees the world through my eyes and I see it in hers. Though she is confined in a porcelain prison, she has escaped the clutches of the underworld. I believe she is content. Her soul and her spirit are free.

To those of you who are just now preparing to go out into the world: Fare well. If the sweet sounds of temptation should visit your dreams do not be afraid to follow. For though it may be the song of the sirens, a life without risk is a life not worth living. Remember that there is always a choice and there are angels among us, watching over us, guiding us and protecting us. Some wear white and bathe in heavenly virtue. Others wear blue velvet.

JOHNNY MOON

Johnny Moon was a lady's man. You could see it in the way he walked – with a glide and a subtle hitch. He was never in a hurry. His smile was a glint in his eyes. The corners of his mouth never turned upward yet he was always smiling. Always.

If tragedy had ever touched the life of Johnny Moon, she never made a mark – at least not anywhere you could see. No one knew how old he was but it seemed certain he was older than he looked. Some of the women he cast aside claimed he was a vampire, sucking the lifeblood from vessels of innocence, yet none but the most naïve could have ever believed that smile belonged to anyone but himself.

When Johnny walked into Stella's Place all eyes turned in wonder. Was tonight the night? Would he play his golden tenor sax? Would he send them home with jazz in their hearts, their souls filled with the sweet nectar of life, a glimpse of perfection, a tribute to the glory of all creation or would he leave them unsatisfied? He had played only twice or thrice in the last several years but it was more than enough to keep his legend alive. The drinks were always free for Johnny Moon. They always would be.

"What'll it be, Johnny?" asked the bartender.

He always asked though the answer was always the same.

"Scotch on the rocks, hold the scotch."

Johnny gave up drinking when he lost the need. As a younger man, he needed the glow that alcohol provided to be the man he wanted to be. He needed it to calm his nerves so he could take the stage and blow. He needed it to give him the courage to approach an unapproachable temptress. He needed it to be Johnny Moon, the man of the hour. He did not need it any more.

He settled on his usual stool at the end of the bar. It gave him a good view of the place and all its inhabitants. It also provided a spotlight. Anyone coming into Stella's found their eyes focused squarely on Johnny and his self-assured grin. Johnny gave you the once-over before your eyes could adjust to bar light.

When Lala appeared at the stage-like entryway, the first thing Johnny noticed was that her eyes did not focus on him. Lala was a gentleman's lady and a fair replica of Johnny's dream woman. Her curves were smooth and flowed like a waterfall. She was not buxom but well proportioned. She moved like a dancer.

Lala felt his eyes warm her body and allowed them to trail her to a corner booth just across the room from Johnny's perch. The bartender abandoned tradition without a second thought, taking an order of two champagnes in tall glasses to her table. He returned with a message for Johnny.

"The lady would like you to join her."

Johnny folded it like a table napkin at an Italian restaurant. He did not like answering to anyone's call. Who does she think he is? A fresh kid with a suitcase of talent and dreams the size of Andromeda? He was Johnny Moon – the Johnny Moon – and Johnny Moon would take his own sweet time.

Still, he ended up at the lady's table, enraptured by her eyes, dark and deep like pools of midnight. The varnished oak shade of her skin was natural. It would not leave pale markings in uncovered places. She wore her hair down, tucked to one side, just like Johnny liked it.

He sat across from her and lost himself in those eyes, those deep pools of darkest mystery. He bathed in her allure. He listened to her slow jazz voice and stripped the cloth from her flesh. For the first time in years, he listened to someone other than himself.

They spoke of life and lessons learned, desire and temptation. They spoke of love, passion and heartache. They spoke of legacy and destiny. They spoke of everything that mattered with a candor that stunned everyone within hearing range. It was a level of openness completely new to Johnny Moon.

She asked him to play. All eyes in the dim lighting turned when he hesitated. This was new ground. One of the few certainties of Stella's was that Johnny did not take requests. He played when the spirit grabbed him, never when asked. Lala, however, was unlike anyone who had ever walked through the door at Stella's refuge for the forlorn. She was a woman used to getting her way and Johnny was in her marks. When he stood, she drew him near with her finger and whispered, "Blue Moon." She teased him with a gentle kiss placed upon his cheek.

"Just for you," Johnny replied.

He walked to the stage and drew out his horn. He fixed his reed, locked eyes with Lala and began to blow. He played like a man reborn, like an artist with the energy of youth and the wisdom of age. He blew like he had never blown before. He reached unreachable notes and pierced their purity with an effortless pulse. He soared to the heights of distant galaxies and dove to the core of being. He discovered new realms of communication, words without words, daggers and darts, feathers and silk, from the heart of darkness to the soul of understanding.

Just when it seemed he was beyond the beyond, he broke seamlessly into Blue Moon – just for Lala. The sorrow that sprang from Johnny's sax filled the room like liquid blues, breaking every heart, and bringing tears of joy and passion to every eye. Johnny Moon was in love and neither man nor woman at that place and time would ever wonder what love is again. Never again would they love a fine red wine or a Hollywood movie. From that moment forward love would be reserved for the divine. Love would belong to that moment when Johnny dove into the void for Lala at Stella's Place.

Johnny held the last note until its reverberation filled the bar and crept out into the street, until the wine glasses joined the serenade with a tingle, sounding like rain, until the last molecule of every living thing felt it to the core, until alas a single tear traced the exquisite brown cheek of Johnny's love.

Lala waited for the silence to settle in the seat of every soul. It was as if nerve gas had been released, leaving its victims breathless, numb and paralyzed. She rose like a glittering star in a sea of stillness and took the stage. She glided to the standing mike with a confidence beyond human bounds, summoning the ghost of Billie Holiday, a goddess in the flesh. When Lala took the stage she owned it. It was clear before she hit her mark, before the spotlight centered, she was no one's second bill. It was clear before her eyes opened, before her lips parted, before her voice was summoned, she possessed the golden touch.

Like a schoolboy with a crush, Johnny took his cue, laying out a melody so soft and tender it would soothe Medea's rage. When Lala sang, men gasped and women wept. Her voice was a timeless vessel for celestial chord. Her song was a message from the goddess, transcending human experience and reaching beyond mortal comprehension. Lala was the archangel of aesthetes, Saint Joan of the soul, and her song recalculated the sum total of knowledge and belief.

No one was touched deeper than Johnny Moon. It was a strange sensation to let go of one's greatness at a ripened age, strange to behold perfection and accept that it is beyond one's reach. Johnny was humbled to the point of weakened knees, shortness of breath and an unsteady gait. As a musician, he had reached his pinnacle, venturing beyond himself, piercing the outer limits of his creative field only to fall in the shadow of Lala's brilliance.

She had been his guide, his inspiration and his muse. She

had opened his eyes, his heart, his every sense. Suddenly, everything he cherished, everything he was or had ever been, everything he dreamed or desired was at her disposal. So pure was his newfound devotion that he was certain as death that he could not go on alone. He would bend himself to her feet. He would become her servant. He would be her protector. He would rip out his heart if need be to demonstrate his loyalty. He would give all he had for the chance to be at her side, to hear her sweet voice, to breathe the same air, to accompany her wherever she might go.

They talked to closing time, asked for a cab and walked out into a deserted city night. Waiting for the cab, Johnny's heart beat so loudly he took deep breaths to calm it. When the cab arrived he opened the door and Lala slipped inside with a sigh.

"I've never met anyone like you," said Johnny.

"Haven't you?" replied Lala with a grin.

"Where are you staying?" he asked.

"I thought I was staying with you," she smiled.

Johnny shuffled in beside her, gave the cabbie directions, and, for a moment, he returned to himself. Once again, he was Johnny Moon, the lady's man, and he had not lost his touch. It seemed that Lala was as taken with him as he was with her.

He was a little embarrassed when he opened the door to his apartment and saw it through her eyes. Johnny was a musician, not a housekeeper, but the least he might have done was to hire a maid to pick up once in a while. Until now it never mattered. He was relieved that Lala did not seem to mind. She took everything in stride. It was almost as though she had been here before and nothing about Johnny could surprise her.

He surprised himself when she turned the conversation to past loves and relationships. In itself, it was not unusual. What was unusual was that Johnny was ready to talk. He had never discussed such things with anyone – particularly not the object of his current attraction. It ran contrary to a well-worn and unwavering philosophy. When it came to Lala, all bets were off. He told her everything and everything flowed from his memory to his conscious mind in startling detail. He recalled the shape of a woman's smile, the sounds she made during love-making, the moves that tantalized his senses, the way she wore her hair, her scent after bathing in the sweat of passion. He remembered hope in the eyes of his lover and the foreshadowing of disappointment, even heartbreak, in the light of the morning sun. Strangely, Lala never spoke of her own history and Johnny never asked.

It was just before dawn when he settled into a deep melancholia, a virtual sea of sighs and silent reflection. His gaze fixed on Lala's enchanting face; he watched her lips curl with satisfaction. Johnny smiled. She rose as if to express her gratitude and her dress seemed to fall from her body of its own will.

She stood before him a portrait of perfection. If her song had been manna from heaven, then this was its nectar. Her scent, her touch, her smile, her heartbeat, replaced all others in his memory. He realized that before this moment he had not known love. He had not known passion. He had never been alive. All else in his lonely existence at once fell flat. Even his music would have no meaning save that which sang her praise.

He awoke in the morning light alone. He called out but no one answered. On the pillow beside him lay a small card:

I am every woman who gave you her love. Remember me, Lala.

Johnny Moon never played again.

TALES FROM BEYOND JAZZTOWN

VISIONS OF RUBY

I am a quiet man. Those who know me by name or reputation alone have told me so. They say I am a man of few words. This is not true. My life is filled with words. Words flow through my mind like a river, relentless and constant. There are so many words within my mind, traveling in so many directions, that I often find it hard to choose. Maybe that is why I choose to speak infrequently. I do not throw my words around to fill the space where thought should be.

I am indeed a quiet man but those who know me know my silence is not empty. It is rich with imagery, vision, sound and rhythm, wonder and reflection. It is not a dark silence but a silence of light. My landscape is not gray but richly colored and textured. Those who inhabit my circle hear my words unspoken. There is no need to speak that which is already known.

When I first met Ruby she was dancing at a bar outside Tuba City in Arizona. I knew at once she understood my unspoken words just as I understood hers. Mine were not difficult to understand. They spoke of her beauty, her grace, and her innocence – yes, her innocence. For even as she shed the layers that passed for modesty, the purity of her untouched, unbroken spirit remained clear as the waters of a virgin spring.

She heard my silent words, my praise and admiration, from across a crowded, overheated barroom, the clouds of lust and dark desire as thick as a desert sandstorm, and from that moment, it was as if she danced only for me. There was nothing dirty about her swirling, writhing, pulsating rhythm, though the crowd of redneck cowboys and goggling natives chortled and hooted with naked abandon. Ruby was pure in her artistry. No Picasso or Beethoven was ever truer to his chosen medium that Ruby was to hers. It reminded me of the snake dance performed with such a delicate touch that all were captivated by her charm. She held my spirit in her hands and allowed me into hers.

Her performance concluded, the gratitude of her admirers collected, I approached her at the bar. She welcomed me as an old friend – as if we had known each other from another life. It was understood: She would tell me her story and I would tell her mine.

Hers was a story of adventure. She skipped over a less that joyful childhood. I understood. Her father was not around. Neither was mine. She traveled around the country – St. Louis, New Orleans, Portland, Seattle, Los Angeles. She finally settled in Las Vegas, a city that appreciated her many talents. Now she was traveling the southwest circuit, hitting strip clubs in Albuquerque, Tucson, Phoenix, Amarillo, and workingman joints in small towns like Tuba City. She told me, with a touch of pride, that she had a steady gig in Vegas any time she wanted it but she liked the adventure of the road.

The explanation was unnecessary. It was as clear as the gleam in her sea green eyes. The spirit of adventure was as much a part of her as the spirit of seeking was a part of me.

She liked not knowing what the morning would bring. She liked saying, "So long, suckers!" any time she wanted. She liked seeing new faces, meeting new people and being open to whatever experience crossed her path. She liked changing scenery and changing partners, though she made it a point that she was highly selective. She gave a wink to that and I could not help but smile with a sense of promise that went bone deep. Ruby lit a fire to my desire like no woman ever has or will. It was understood.

More than anything, Ruby loved the road. She loved the

dotted arrow and the rhythm of the telephone lines. She loved looking at life framed in a windshield or a rearview mirror. She loved the wind in her hair and motel showers, gas stations and highway rest stops. She loved truck stops and biker bars. She loved it all.

When she had gone as far as she wanted to go, I confided that I already knew her. I told her I was an inhabitant of two worlds, each with many levels and dimensions of existence. I knew her from another world, another dimension, where she alone was queen. She laughed a tender laugh as if it was just sweet talk and she was letting me off the hook, but I knew that she knew I was sincere.

We went for a moonlight drive in her baby blue convertible. We roamed the high desert mesa, where the land has a snow-like glow and every rock formation, every outcropping, every crevice, canyon and sagebrush, everything takes on a new life, a spirit life unto itself.

"This is the way of the desert," I said. "It teaches you that all things are spirit and that everything, from the smallest stone to the Grand Canyon, must be treasured and treated with respect."

"It's the same everywhere," she replied. "If your eyes are open and you know where to look, every place is Disneyland!"

We laughed and shared our thoughts in silence, following a dirt path to the edge of Red Bluff Canyon, where we parked under a sky of a million stars, so close you could leap up and join in their dance. There, beneath the majesty of Father Sky, before the wonder of Mother Earth, I decided to share with her the sacred seeds of my ancestors. I had saved them for just such an occasion. One does not take lightly the taking of the sacred seed. To my people, it is a deeply religious experience.

Ruby laughed but she understood the honor and the reverence required. She had taken many of the white man's spiritual medicines but never with reverence, never with the purity of spirit that was being asked of her now.

I said a prayer and we began the path to the spiritual world. We made our way to a ledge that seemed perched over the heart of the canyon. There we sat to watch, in full and tempting silence, the translation of one mystical reality into another. Before our eyes, straining with delight, everything seemed to accelerate and intensify. We came to realize that we were sitting on a living, breathing, pulsing being, this great sphere of stone, fire, water and soil, rolling through open space, this giver of life, this earth our mother.

We pressed our bodies together and held on for fear that we might lose our grasp and be thrust into that emptiness from which none returns. We held onto each other for fear of being lost in forever darkness, alone.

The earth rushed in its revolution through space. The stars and the moon above streaked across the heavens. We had stepped out of time. The desert life forms came and went: life and death, hunting and killing, dying and decaying. Man-made structures, monstrous towers of concrete and steel, sprang from the desert floor and crumbled into dust.

A voice, at first distant and then, ever closer, spoke to us. *Was it the voice of our mother, the voice of the stars, or the voice of all being all knowing?* We knew only that it spoke to us, clinging to each other like frightened children, and it hailed the sanctity of the one. It praised the sanctity of the two becoming one, the yin and yang, the spirit and its opposing spirit, the man and the woman. It spoke in words that cannot be translated but the meaning was clear and confident: One man, one woman, together in love, is more precious and rare than all of human kind's treasures and accomplishments. The sanctuary of love gives meaning to all we experience. There is no greater truth than this.

We were joined in heavenly embrace, merged into one being, dancing with the stars to one beat, joined to the earth and the heavens. We let go of all other thoughts and of thought itself, expanding, floating and sinking at once. We were locked in a love so far beyond ourselves we became one with all without ourselves. We lost ourselves willingly and with eyes wide open. We touched the heartbeat of the force of all being and let it take us to a distant space where sacred waters sang and skies, flowered with flowing colors, bathed and soothed our souls.

We lost consciousness, lost all bearing, lost awareness of what must have transpired in the passage of time. I awakened on the canyon floor, crude voices assaulting my ears. Someone poked me with a stick.

"Get up, Injun Joe! Your girlfriend wants you!"

A beast of a man, with full beard and frazzled hair, held Ruby in his arms, limp and lifeless. She moaned as I struggled to my feet. The beast's companions, two smaller men, dusted and dirty, cackled like fowl and shuffled their feet. This was their idea of fun in the desert. I reached for my knife but it was gone. One of the men brandished it, baring his decayed teeth.

For reasons I could not then understand, I had no fear. I had communed with the land, with the earth and the sky. I had joined with Ruby in a dance of the divine. I had acquired the blessings of the Great Spirit and all things living and breathing in the sacred world were my brothers and sisters.

"Let her go," I quietly demanded.

Their laughter reverberated in the canyon, thunder in my skull, and the earth began to move beneath my feet. I watched terror enter their souls (yes, even worms have souls) as their eyes were fixed to mine. In the reflection of the big man's eyes, I saw myself transformed. I was the wolf and bared my fangs with a growl.

Was I the wolf or was it an illusion? If it was an illusion, it was shared by four sentient beings.

I started forward and the beast immediately dropped Ruby and, in one motion, ran for his life, his companions trailing like hyenas from a fierce predator. They would never again see an Indian with the same eyes. They would never again confront strangers in the desert without fear.

Ruby awakened and watched their retreat up the north canyon wall. In their haste, they left two burros behind.

"What happened?" she wondered.

"They were spooked by the desert winds," I replied.

She shook her head and kissed my hand as I helped her to her feet. We discarded their belonging – shovels, picks, supplies – and rode the burros back to the car. We set the animals free. They could return to their grizzly human partners or not. It was their choice.

We spent the day recovering at my cabin on the mesa. Ruby was a mystique. She tossed the I Ching, consulted the stars and mused on numerology. She said that I was a man of independent spirit. She said that we were forever linked.

I asked her to stay but she had a gig in Winslow. The road beckoned. I kissed her goodbye and we left unspoken the promise to meet again. We would leave it to the stars, the moon, the earth and the four winds.

I watched her vanish into the desert night, her hair dyed to seven shades of green, leaving behind a trail of glowing light. She left behind as well a heart filled with longing and a spirit filled with wonder.

As I let her beauty wash over me, I knew she was not of this world. I would always remember and cherish the thought: Every man should be so blessed to have a vision of Ruby in the desert skyline.

WILD MAN OF ALBUQUERQUE

"PEACE TO YOU!" he shouts in parting.

It is his usual response to the poetry reading peaceniks at the Café Royal, just down from the university and the Frontier Restaurant, in the heart of the student district, on a midsummer Wednesday night.

He has listened to their endless lamentations, their testimonials of compassion for the homeless, the forgotten, the veterans of war, the displaced and discarded souls of the ever-expanding universe.

Tonight he has listened, just as he has listened countless times before, with open mind, hoping to find some glimmer of truth, a genuine insight, a pearl within the sea of posturing dribble. The romantic, the empathetic, the radical, all spewing strings of sound, competing for entry into what they perceive as higher circles of artistic accomplishment. Their words are as empty as an atheist's prayers – for effect only.

Tonight he listens until he can listen no longer, until the beast within erupts in a tirade of protest. It is not unexpected. The local bicycle patrol is on hand, providing a swift and peaceful escort down the road to the repeated incantation, "Peace to YOU!"

He is the Wild Man of Albuquerque. He is the subject, the heart and soul, of their creative angst, yet they can scarcely look him in the eyes. They fear him just as they fear the cold indifference of their own lives, the truths beneath the surface of their daily routines.

They read the underground rags, watch the X Files, listen to hip hop and rap, burn incense and sage, attend powwows, sweats and Sun Dances, and rage against the machine in the safe circle of their peers, all to appease the gods in which they no longer believe, all to stake their claim as the chosen ones who bear no blame for the destruction of the environment, for the injustices of the privileged class, for the excesses of police and government authority, when it all comes down. When the revolution finally hits the streets, they will be allowed to pass. They will be allowed to carry on just as they have always done, under the cloak of artistic freedom.

"Peace to YOU!" the Wild Man yells in parting, as the bicycle cops, in Khaki shorts and so cool mirror shades, chase him back into the shadow from which he came.

A plot is hatched at one of the outdoor tables of the Café Royal, where a trio of poets, sipping lattes, has observed the usual confrontation and quietly sided with the outcast.

"Let's follow him," says Hawk. The elder of the three and fresh out of Chicago with a radical edge, he is granted the credibility of unknown experience and worldliness. He is the leader and will remain so until his leadership betrays them.

"Why?" ponders Redge. She is the younger, a student of cultural diversity and mixed fashion, with a buzz cut and tie-dye baggies. Some within the circle of poets call her "Chrissie" – an allusion to The Pretenders. Others call her "Wanna" – as in "want to be" – but she prefers "Redge" for the father she knows only in name.

"Grist for the mill," answers Wolf, a large bearded man with longish dark hair. He is a native and the progeny of the children of the sixties, who landed here when their VW busses broke down, threw a rod, on their way to Shangri-La (AKA, Haight-Ashbury circa 1969). His poetry is considered substandard but his spirit and his rap – especially in praise of other poets – is appreciated.

Wolf is pleased to observe that he has answered correctly, pleased to be on the winning side, and pleased to catch the wave of Hawk's thought. He remains behind to deposit cash on the table as Hawk and Redge hustle to catch the Wild Man's trail. Heaving and panting, Wolf joins them at a corner where the Wild Man has turned and headed for the outskirts of town.

Hawk gestures for Wolf to pant more quietly and they wait for a safe distance. They do not want to be detected. To be detected would force their hand. They would have to join the Wild Man, risking alienation of the poetry circle, or abandon him, risking serious damage to their perception of themselves as poets on the edge. Both are consequences they would go to great lengths to avoid.

They proceed at a more leisurely pace, a pace they believe would allow them the explanation (however flawed or specious) that they are simply on a stroll to gather in the vibes of the desert sunset.

The Wild Man, hunched shoulders, walks on at a dedicated pace, oblivious to his followers, his wild hair dancing the wind, a silhouette of Medusa in the evening light. Not once does he look behind. Not once does he appear to suspect that someone would be interested enough to follow him, as he has followed others beneath the shadows of the night.

They watch in amazement as the Wild Man gathers a bundle of envelopes from his mailbox and enters what was once a motor home—long past it vehicular status. What passes for his yard is crowded with potted cacti, bundles of sage and such, and objects of art.

As they gain confidence that their espionage will not be discovered, Hawk leads them closer until they huddle together at the far end of the motor home, where they share whispered observations of atonement for their misconceptions regarding the Wild Man of Albuquerque. They are stunned that this man, with no visible means of support, with no sense of fashion or cleanliness, an outcast treated with disdain by his peers and his community, not only has a home but a life, replete with correspondence and an appreciation of art. Who knows but that he may even be the artist!

But their sense of awe is dwarfed by what happens now, as the almost mythological sound of a mechanical typewriter at full speed emerges from the motor home and fills the space of their huddled consciousness.

"He's a writer!" says Hawk in the hushed tones usually reserved for the likes of Ginsberg and Kerouac. The revelation settles slowly, like the airing of a fine wine.

The Wild Man pounds furiously at his machine, sending a cacophony of letters, sounds, words, into the desert night before unleashing the completed work and pausing for a moment's reflection. It seems an eternity but only a few minutes have passed, leaving the unmistakable mark of true inspiration, that most rare of creative qualities, in its wake.

"From the gods through the machine!" whispers Wolf.

"He's a channeler," adds Redge.

"From the infinite depths of the creative all force / to the spiritual essence of the Wild Man of Albuquerque / through the humble Remington / to the virgin tablet of the printed page," intones Hawk.

The door opens and the Wild Man, crunching an apple and looking strangely unaltered, emerges, transferring a dark object from his hand to the inside pocket of his coat.

"It's a gun!" says Redge.

This throws a new wrinkle into the evening's adventure. Following a wild man poet is one thing but following a wild man poet with a gun is quite another.

Hawk is committed to carrying on but Wolf has a new idea. He wants to read the Wild Man's inspiration, to examine his life from the inside, to explore his creative works. Redge remains silent, undecided. They are at a crossroads and Hawk, sensing the threat, quickly devises a compromise.

"We'll follow him," he says. "You stay here and scope it out. When he comes back, we'll give you a warning. Three caws of the crow and get the hell out of here."

They agree, though Redge's hesitation suggests that she would rather stay behind with Wolf. Wolf promises to write down the inspired work and they move off before the Wild Man is beyond following. Wolf watches as Redge strains to keep up and laughs quietly: Redge following Hawk following the Wild Man back into the shadowed streets of Albuquerque. He is worried for them – especially Redge. The most adventurous thing she has done up to now is trying nutmeg on her cappuccino. No matter. He has his mission and his heart is pounding as he crosses the threshold into the Wild Man's abode.

"Hurry up!" Hawk orders. His patience is waning. It is a long, harried walk – beyond the well-lighted, relatively safe streets of the university section, across the tracks, to the darkened streets on the other side, where the nightlife of Albuquerque is happening. It is a world of bars, bikers, hip-hop, drug dealing, cross dressers and whores. It is a world of back alleyways and dark enclaves where anything can happen and often does.

Redge is about to give up and start the long walk back when the Wild Man settles by a corner and watches the street life. It is an endless parade of cultural diversity, a study in the struggle for individual expression, and they begin to see it from the Wild Man's eyes.

The wait is just long enough for them to gather themselves and catch their breath. Suddenly, the Wild Man springs to his feet and darts down the street, turning once and then again, into a dark alley where three large men in leather confront a woman with heavy mascara, teased red hair, and a short, tight dress. One has a knife. Redge hesitates to go any further and Hawk pulls up. They fold into the darkness and watch.

The Wild Man walks into the center of the action and wields his weapon. He orders the men to leave her alone and backs them off. Hawk, having second thoughts but not wanting to seem a coward in front of Redge, starts toward them. The Wild Man is distracted, looking over his shoulder, just long enough to lose his advantage. He takes a knife to the gut. His gun is kicked out of his hand.

Redge and Hawk stand aghast as the Wild Man of Albuquerque lay bleeding on the pavement. The leathers are gone. The sound of a siren in the distance startles them and the woman in the short dress takes refuge in the night. Hawk approaches the Wild Man and kneels at his side.

"Peace to you," he whispers and coughs.

The Wild Man is dying, Hawk decides. Redge is pleading, "Let's get out of here! Let's get out of here!"

"Peace to you," says Hawk in parting.

They make their way back to the motor home, where Wolf has filled a small notebook with the Wild Man's muse.

"He's dead," says Hawk.

The next day he reads about it in the paper. The Wild Man is not dead. The Wild Man survives. The Wild Man will always survive. He survives to remind us that life is real. He is real. His message is clear: That the path to true expression is one of flesh, blood and marrow – not one of words. Words can have no greater meaning than the experience behind them.

The Wild Man of Albuquerque is not surprised to hear his own words at the Café Royal one summer's evening. He is not surprised to be published in a local rag. He is not surprised at the praise and the accolades.

"Peace to you," he says in passing.

"Peace to you."

FATAL FLAW

Driving along a blue highway, Nashville to Austin parallel the interstate, a hitchhiker rolls into view and quickly shrinks into the rearview mirror. I am reminded of the forlorn days when I was the hitchhiker vanishing in the rearview mirror. I am reminded that I am still the hitchhiker. I have always been the hitchhiker. It was a role that attracted me like a primordial instinct, like an ancient memory in the deep pockets of my mind.

I am the hitchhiker.

I have always been the hitchhiker.

In this life, I calculate that I have logged over fifteen thousand miles, guided always by a subliminal destiny far beyond the town at the end of a ride.

The pinnacle of my digital sojourn was my first cross-country run. Teamed with a veteran of the road (a kid five years my elder, whom I had met doing summer theatre in my hometown), we covered the continent in three and a half days – that after spending eighteen hours on the exit ramp to Mustang Ranch, the infamous legal house of prostitution near Reno, Nevada. Stranded by a drunken gambler intent on spending his winnings or easing the pain of his losses, I came to a decision on that lonesome two-lane highway that would become a guiding light for the rest of this life on earth.

My partner, expecting (with good cause) my deference to his seniority, announced his intention to walk back to Reno. I refused outright. Don't turn back. It was a golden rule and one that I sensed as if it was wired into my spine. We went our separate ways but my determination turned out the stronger. He caught up with me on my eastward trek, where a trucker picked us up after a mile or two.

In those days, truckers never picked up hitchhikers – at least, not our kind of freewheeling, Highway 61, long hair, patched Levi types. We had a rating system for vehicles according to the probability of them giving up a ride. Volkswagen busses were gold. Eighteen-wheelers and rigs were dog meat – as bad as a Rolls Royce.

Being picked up by a trucker on a high-speed, two-lane highway in hitchhiker hell was the closest thing to a miracle I had ever experienced. A ride out of Winnemucca took us nonstop across the Mississippi. It was a rare glimpse of atonement, a sensation of accomplishment and exhilaration. It was far too cool for words.

At the opposite end of the spectrum, the black hole of my hitchhiking experience was when I gave it up on a New York to California run and took the bus in from Flagstaff, Arizona. I ran out of energy. I ran out of money. I ran out of faith. I was defeated and felt like crawling into a cocoon to await an uncertain transformation.

A friend had a running joke about hitchhiking: I was hungry and you gave me food. I was thirsty and you gave me water. I was cold and you gave me shelter. But when I was stranded by the roadside in Winnemucca, you passed me by.

I was nearing the end of my hitchhiking days. The world had changed and I had adapted inward, no longer willing to put it all on the line or to risk exposure in an unfamiliar environment. I erected the appropriate barriers, sat back, and listened to Pink Floyd's *The Wall* for a hundred years before I awakened.

All that was before the hitchhiker died. No one knows when it happened but we all know that it came to pass. Those who roam the highways and blue roads now are desperados without horses, without the honor or nobility that legend and history give such characters. The true adventurers, the seekers, the journeyers, the pilgrims, are nowhere to be found. They vanished with the old

Volkswagen busses, constructed with a fatal flaw: A thrown rod was like a spear through the heart of its sputtering, feeble engine.

So now, when I see a hitchhiker, it sends me reeling, twisting in a sacred spiral of confusion and lost innocence, propelling beyond a glorious past into a future of endless gray. What was the fatal flaw that threw a rod into the heart of a generation?

Now, when I see a hitchhiker, I no longer see myself. I see a villain, a threat, a challenge to my secure vision of the world, and I mourn that loss of innocence. How I longed to be lost in the daze of Woodstock, in the haze of fallen heroes, in the holy wasteland of my youth.

All these thoughts run through my head, like the flash of an Einstein insight, every time I pass a hitchhiker by – or rather, what passes for a hitchhiker today.

Not this time. This time I turn back. I pull off the road, spin around, and watch the hitchhiker's features change. The thrill of a ride survives. He is a younger man, in his late twenties to early thirties, with a scruffy beard and scraggly hair, dressed in dungarees, Army boots, and wearing a John Deere baseball cap. He is a man who does not know how to thank the memory of Woodstock for his good fortune.

He jumps in the car and accepts a ride all the way to Austin. A couple of miles runs out the stilted conversation, supplanting it with an air of tension. A couple more miles and a crooked, deer-hunting grin takes over him. He brandishes his courage in a blade of steel...

I was the hitchhiker and the hitchhiker is dead. No one knows when it happened or why but we all know how. He took a rod through the heart when he forgot the golden rule: Don't turn back.

BURNING CHURCHES

"It is not the temperature," the Major said in a lazy drawl so pronounced only a fellow Southerner would lend it credibility. "It is not the temperature," he repeated for no other reason than that he derived pleasure from the sensation as the word *temperature* rolled off his tongue, slow and clinging like Georgia molasses.

"It is not the temperature, it is the viscosity."

He puffed what remained of his Cuban cigar and blew the smoke in concentric circles that hovered in the hot, viscous air. It was a vile habit and one that he embraced with all his southern pride. Hot. Damnably hot. But from where he sat on the porch of a century old cabin overlooking the Great Smokey Mountains, it might have been heaven. You could tell by the way he fidgeted in his rocker that the Major was feeling frisky.

Cousin Billy Bob, a young man of the transitional age when it was only slightly impolite to address him as a boy, stood in camouflage khakis bearing a message of good news. He could only smile in appreciation of the Major's witticism. It was only slightly over his head.

Billy Bob was what the culture made of William Robert Moss. He was not the Major's cousin but, then, the Major was not a Major. It was a term of endearment more or less. He was here to deliver a progress report on the organization's master plan. His report was primarily responsible for the Major's good humor.

The organization was neither the Klan nor Klan related. The Klan was old news, forever grounded in the past. Theirs was an organization with its eyes set dead ahead. They were well-respected men at the top of their games, collecting converts more rapidly than Baptist missionaries in the Congo. They were businessmen, politicians, lawyers, civil servants, artists, artisans, writers, musicians, clerks, accountants, sportsmen, hikers, survivalists, religious zealots and atheists. In short, they were every mother's son with one distinction: They were all white.

***

"We are all God's children!" the preacher cried out in the distinctive cadence made famous by the likes of Reverend Ike, Jesse Jackson and Martin Luther King. "We are all God's children – black, white, brown, yellow and red – united as one people in the eyes of our Lord and comforted in the hands of our Savior, Jesus of Nazareth."

The Reverend William James Jackson was known as Willie Jay to his congregation of just under one hundred in one of the better sections of the small town of Waynesborough, North Carolina. They were the more fortunate of the greater community of African Americans, well respected, socially involved, and financially secure if not truly affluent. Several decades removed from the direct effects of racial discrimination, they had grounded their economic well-being in the black community and conscientiously repaid the community with job development, charitable contributions, rehabilitation centers, and active participation in the schools, local government and churches.

The subject of the good Reverend's sermon did not surprise them. For months it had been a dominant theme: The burning of churches with predominantly or exclusively black congregations. The latest count was in the eighties nation wide, but the vast majority were south of the Mason-Dixon line. They had established a relief fund and some of their members had traveled hundreds of miles to assist in rebuilding not only churches but also faith in the greater society of human kind.

They were not surprised but they did not expect the hateful phenomenon – a legacy of racial violence, intolerance and bigotry – to come home.

***

The Major was spearheading a special project for an organization that, for all practical purposes, did not exist. They had no official meetings. They elected no officers. They collected no dues. They did not publish a newsletter and their business was rarely conducted over any medium. When it was it was carefully coded. Anonymity and secrecy were of paramount concern.

It all began in the smoking room at one of the many black tie gala events to which his wife was devoted. He adored his wife and, after the expected period of pleading and protestation, he always consented to attend. The truth was his social life was severely limited since his retirement from the army with the rank of Lieutenant Colonel. He enjoyed these formal gatherings almost as much as she did.

On this particular occasion, a very distinguished gentleman – a former District Attorney – was commenting on the crime situation, with the not so subtle implication that those of darker complexion were responsible for making the streets unsafe. He lamented at some length the exorbitant costs of adequate security – an absolute necessity even and especially in the finest of neighborhoods.

"It is unfortunate," the Major finally replied, "that the race war of the late sixties never fully materialized. We might have exterminated half of them and sent the other half back to the Dark Continent."

It was a shocking comment and an almost unforgivable breech of etiquette at a social affair – even when confined to the smoking room. Within minutes, of course, it circulated throughout the gathering and within days, naturally, it had permeated much of the state, giving the Major an indelible reputation as a man of integrity.

Owing partly to his virtue of drinking to excess at such affairs, he was forgiven by his social peers and he had made his first converts. In the coming months, he discovered that he had made many more. The secret society grew and prospered. It seemed the mood of the country and the South was at last ripe.

***

The Reverend cast his line, set his jig, and settled back on his haunches, letting the boat drift slowly in the shallows of the pond. It was well stocked with catfish and smallmouth bass, but it was not the fishing that kept Willie Jay coming back to the pond like clockwork every Monday morning. It was the time with his trusted companion, friend and the sole employee of the Missionary Baptist Church that he valued.

Jackie Robinson Brown was a former prizefighter, a Golden Glove champion, who had once contended for the bantamweight crown. He still carried the 1949 Ring Magazine that listed his name among the top ten contenders and showed it to anyone who politely expressed an interest.

Jackie, himself, had lost interest in almost everything after the death of his wife and only child in a freak automobile accident. He was wandering the streets begging for loose change (unacceptable behavior in Waynesborough), when the Reverend took him under his wing. In his younger days, Willie Jay was both a fight fan and a gambling man. He had won a fair amount of pocket money betting on the local pugilistic hero and he considered it the work of God that he was in a position to repay him with an honest job and shelter.

For the past twelve years, Jackie had been the janitor at the finest African American church in town. He was proud of his position, proud of his relationship with the Reverend

Willie Jay, and he took pride in his work. Many were the nights he would sleep on a cot in the church loft, too tired to make the trek home. Or maybe he just liked being close to God.

"Got me a nibbler," Jackie whispered, one eye on his jig and the other on Willie Jay. He was a fine fisherman and he was proud of that too. He enjoyed Monday mornings as much as the Reverend did.

Willie Jay watched him grasp his rod with the delicate touch of a surgeon. The jig darted in the still water and Jackie jerked his rod back and reeled it in with the smile of a seven-year-old who just hit a home run in little league baseball. He admired his catch briefly. It was a keeper – a fourteen-inch cat – but he released it back into the pond, as was his habit. Willie Jay accused him of catching the same fish over and over but he could never prove it. In all these many years, he had kept only a handful and those he gave away to people "less fortunate than myself."

"You haven't mentioned the sermon." The Reverend waited before breaching the subject. They always touched on the Sunday sermon as a starting point to general discussions on the meaning of life and the state of human affairs. It was traditional for Jackie to initiate the discussion but on this Monday morning, he fell silent.

"Not much to say," he replied after a time to punctuate his consternation. "You been givin' that same sermon for five weeks now."

"They're burning churches, Jackie! Our churches!"

They had been through this before but the Reverend never gave up trying to bend Jackie to his views, despite the immutable fact that Jackie's opinions were set in something more solid than granite – namely, true conviction. The only individual in the county more obstinate than Jackie was the Reverend Willie Jay, himself.

"The Lord don't see it that way."

"You got a pipeline to the Lord, do you?"

RANDOM JACK

The Reverend knew it was a mistake as soon as he said it. Jackie would not respond to the semantic traps Willie Jay so often set. He would just roll his eyes as he was doing now.

"Don't do no good stirring up trouble," Jackie said finally, putting a cap on their discussion of the Sunday sermon. As it turned out, it was a good day for fishing – just fishing.

***

The Major was preparing for a reunion of Army buddies in Detroit. As a matter of policy, he always arranged a social engagement during an operation – especially one in his region of the country.

It was carefully planned to appear unplanned: The reckless, drunken act of a couple of kids. A generous amount of whiskey would be found on the premises. None would be hurt. It was not their intention to kill. They only wanted to stir things up, to ignite the racial tension that was as much southern heritage as Old Hickory and Robert E. Lee. If it spread to the rest of the country so much the better. Unlike previous periods of unrest, this time they would be prepared for what followed.

The days of affirmative action were graciously coming to a close. The welfare nation would soon be history. Poverty was an indelible fact. That it affected more black Americans than white was a fact open to interpretation. When the proverbial crap hit the fan, two communities would be armed and ready: drug pushers and survivalists. Handcuffed though they might be, the Major figured he could count on the government to enter the fray on their side. It was his job to make sure his people were better armed than the enemy was.

He provided cousin Billy Bob with the names and addresses of two local boys and a map of Waynesborough. It would take place between two and three in the morning – just after the Major checked in to a Detroit hotel.

***

Monday was Jackie's day off. On occasion, however, when he was feeling restless, after fishing and an afternoon nap, he would put in a few hours of work to take the edge off whatever was troubling him. On this particular Monday he was feeling restless. Fishing could be hard time when it was just fishing. He could not quite get a grip on it – which was why it would not leave him in peace. Of course he wanted to help. Who wouldn't? It was something else: a sense of foreboding, unease, maybe a premonition. It was as if he had been through this before.

He was three generations removed from the scourge of slavery. He had spent his share of time in the cotton fields, on the backs of busses, and in the shantytowns of the segregated South. He had gone from colored to Negro to black to Afro to African American. He had lived through the civil rights movement, the assassinations, black pride, the Nation of Islam, Black Panthers and the first race war. He was boxing out of Chicago when the streets went up in flames and all hell broke loose. He was not then politically aware but he was caught in the crossfire and neither the police nor the National Guard was asking which side you were on. If you were on the streets and you were black, you were the enemy.

He survived but not without casualty. He spent three days in the hospital and three years paying for it. At the time, he considered himself fortunate because, if he had still been standing, they would have taken him to jail. As it was, his boxing career was over and with it his dream of a better life for his children all but died. His life was turned head over feet.

Now Jackie smelled trouble. Big trouble. The same kind of trouble he sensed way back when in Chicago. The last thing he wanted was another race war. Nothing good would come of it. He did not know, however, how to deal with the sort of people who made sport of burning churches.

It was late in the evening by the time he glanced at his watch. His mind had been racing so swiftly he did not notice the time until he realized he had waxed and polished every bench in the worship hall. He was suddenly drained and took only a moment to decide: he would not make the walk home. He turned out the lights, climbed the stairs to the loft, and quickly fell asleep.

***

Jimmy and Braden were the sons of good old boys. They shared a lot in life. They played sports, liked pretty girls, cold beer, hot cars and country music. They graduated from high school with mediocre grades and virtually no job skills – unless you counted auto mechanics, which had nothing whatsoever to do with the high school curriculum.

They were both well trained in the ways of good old boys by the examples of their fathers – an amazing feat when you consider their fathers were gone by the time they were seven years old. They were best friends, roommates, and they knew exactly what life had in store for them. So when they were offered an opportunity for a little off-the-road excitement, while serving a cause they vaguely believed in, forging a connection with what they considered the big boys and picking up some serious spending money, they jumped on it like fleas on a sleeping dog.

They were the grunts of the organization and it did not bother them. They were well groomed. They knew no names, no faces, and no phone numbers. They were contacted through a vendor at a traveling gun show. They knew only to expect a man wearing a Confederate ball cap near the witching hour.

Cousin Billy Bob arrived exactly at two o'clock, shook hands, and laid out the plan. Everything they needed –

gloves, ski masks, two bottles of whiskey, six Molotov cocktails – were in the back of his truck. There were windows on both sides of the building. The boys would hit each side with two cocktails apiece, while he took care of the front. The structure was constructed of bricks but the interior and roofing was all wood. It would go up like a bed of dry pine boughs.

"It's hit and run, boys. We don't stand around to admire the work."

The last thing Billy Bob told them was what to say in the event they were caught: They were drinking and they did it on a dare. The cocktails were kerosene with white rags torn from tee shirts and dipped in kerosene. They learned how to make them from a TV show. The kerosene was already in the house for camping supplies. If Billy Bob was caught with them, he was just someone they met at the Sunday flea market who stayed over. If not, he did not exist. Anything else they could not remember or did not know.

When everything seemed clear enough they each took a hit of whiskey and got under way, like three secret agents on a mission in Moscow, too young, too ignorant or too dazed to see the folly of their own footsteps.

***

"Doggone kids!" Jackie said as he sat up, flipped on the lamp, glanced at the clock, and wondered if it was worth the effort.

It was unusual in this part of town but, during the summer months, an occasional act of youthful vandalism was not unexpected. He had been through it before. *They'll be long gone by the time I ...* That's when he smelled burning wax and kerosene and fear gripped his gut.

He heard the front door being kicked in as he coaxed his legs to the door of the loft. He knew from the sound of erupting fire what he would see when he opened it. There

100

was no way out. The small window in the loft was barred for security. He opened the door and confirmed the nightmare. The fresh wax acted as tinder. The entire church was filled from floor to rafters with the flames of racial hatred.

***

The sound of a man's screams when his body is engulfed in flames is terrifying. It touches a raw nerve. It sends a chill down the spine and sets hair on end. What begins as horror is soon supplanted by a sickening feeling, bone deep, that makes a man want to cry and regurgitate at the same time.

Jimmy did neither. He stopped on a dime and tore off his ski mask. Braden made it almost to the truck when Jimmy cried out.

"Shit! That's Jackie, man!"

Cousin Billy Bob was enraged, his face beet red beneath his mask. He was pissed that they had miscalculated, pissed that there was a man in the church, pissed that the Major would surely blame this on him, pissed that they had set him up with a couple of losers, but mostly he was pissed that they were still there.

"Get in the damned truck!"

Jimmy looked straight into Braden's eyes. "It's Jackie!" he repeated.

Jackie Robinson Brown was more than a local sports hero to the boys of Waynesborough. In a series of community outreach programs he had taught many of them how to box. Jimmy and Braden were among them. Jackie was the one African American they liked and respected. Even their fathers had called him "a credit to his race."

Jimmy delayed no longer. He dashed into the burning church, tears clouding his vision and judgment almost as much as the smoke and fire. Braden waited a few moments longer.

"Get in the goddamned truck!"

By the time Braden reached the front doors of the church, the fire and heat were so intense it nearly knocked him to the ground. It was too late. His best friend and the town's hero were both surely dead. The truck was gone. He heard Jimmy's scream just as they heard Jackie's before. He stumbled to the lawn of the church, collapsed and wept as a baby plucked from his mama's breast, until the firemen and police arrived.

***

Braden still wept when the Reverend Willie Jay arrived. When he heard the story and learned of his friend's horrible death, he wanted to relinquish his theological oath and batter this boy to submission. But he took one look at the sobbing, stuttering youth and his tears were joined to the offender's.

He realized that God's punishment was swift, indeed, and that the survivor of this tragedy was the most unfortunate of all. In all the years of his still young life, he would never recover from the tormenting, haunting stain of his unwitting part in this drama.

No threats, no deals, no lengthy interrogation was required. Braden opened like a field of wildflowers in morning light and all he knew came spilling forth. He provided an accurate description of cousin Billy Bob and the Chevy pickup truck he drove. He identified the gun dealer and remembered just enough of the Chevy's license number to track down its owner.

Billy Bob was stopped at a gas station before he could get home where one the Major's cleanup agents was waiting. They had heard the news and they would take no chances on Billy Bob ending up in the hands of the law. They had not misjudged the extent of his loyalty but they never expected him to face a charge of murder.

After two days of questioning, two days of dealing with

an unsympathetic public defender, and not a word from the Major, Billy Bob gave it up. The Major would take the fall.

The last rites of Jackie Robinson Brown were a fitting tribute to a great man who accepted a modest role in life. It was one of the best-attended funerals in the county's history. People from all over the country – including the families of two misguided youths – came to pay their respects to the man who had touched so many hearts. The Reverend Willie Jay reflected that it was little compensation for the absence he felt and would always feel in the pit of his soul – but it was at least some consolation and it would have to do.

The Major took the honorable way out. His veiled wife and two members of the immediate family attended his funeral.

DIXIE FREEZE

The storm hit on Winter Solstice, the longest night of the year. Snow turned to rain and rain turned to ice, covering sidewalks and roads, collecting on wires, limbs and branches. From behind an open window in the comfort of a warm living room the beauty is breathtaking.

It sounds like a war zone. The sudden freeze compresses metal, glass and wood, causing transformers to explode like mortars. Wires and water pipes snap, branches crack and whole trees lose their grounding.

The initial aesthetic of a winter wonderland is lost in the grim vision of the morning after. The roads are impassable, power is down and panic grips the city. The rush to get supplies, food and water is on. Vehicles of every description are abandoned on the roadside, in bogs and ditches, and the usual criminal element is in action, stealing anything left unguarded.

That was six weeks ago, before the ice returned to snow and the snow kept falling and falling and falling. I was in the city when the storm hit, consuming my sorrow in a sea of Christmas spirits, toasting my newfound liberty. My divorce was final. I was officially alone – except for the dogs. All I could think about was getting home.

Nashville is ill equipped for snow, no less an ice storm. There are not enough salt trucks, not enough plows and not enough experience in emergency management. I had to get home while I still could.

Home is in the country ten miles out of town. Looking back, in my little Mercury without chains, it was a borderline miracle I made it. Now, five feet of snow later, I wondered if

I made the right choice. In town at least there is a relief effort and others to share the burden. Then again, I have the dogs to think about.

The outdoor dogs, one resembling a wolf and the other the lone survivor of a litter of three, might have been able to get by but Sadie, a border collie mix with the spirit of a champion, would have been trapped inside. All have suffered some degree of abandonment. It's a common bond and I'm determined it will not happen again.

There's no means of communication – no link to the outside world. It's a time for introspection, a time for contemplating the direction of my life, a time to acknowledge failures and rediscover success. It's not a time for delusions or mindless amusement. It's pointless to muse without someone to be amused.

The neighbors are of little value. They stopped by several times in the early going with the latest reports they gleaned from a battery-powered radio: endless theories on global climate change and dire predictions of a new ice age. Scientists are scrambling for explanations to the suddenness of change and its worldwide scope: A tilt in the planet's axis, a cosmic radiation storm, solar flares, an interaction of industrial pollutants and extraterrestrial elements. As the days wear on the explanations grow incomprehensible and all but irrelevant. The reports always seemed to end with: We just don't know.

A back-to-earth couple a little older than me, the neighbors are making plans. In the beginning, it was all about unity and survival in a frozen wilderness but when the chill of reality set in and the prospect of a made-for-TV movie dimmed, they got out while there was still time. They were heading south but beyond that, they had not decided on a destination.

I might have gone with them but I had the dogs to think about and a vision of being stranded somewhere in a sea of snow with no one to hunker down with but them gave me pause. They're good people, generous and kind enough, but they bring with them a strange mix of Tennessee country and new age communalism. They perceive themselves as some brand of spiritual leaders and I'm not of a mind to follow.

In a gesture of goodwill that seemed melodramatic at the time, they left me a .22 rifle, a box of bullets and a couple boxes of canned goods. I was grateful and as the snow continued to fall with each passing day, my sense of gratitude deepened.

The last word I got came from a sheriff on a snowmobile. He said looters had cleaned out all the stores in the city and marauders were beginning to roam the countryside. He asked if I had a gun and left the impression I might have to use it. He told me the law was breaking down, officers and soldiers disbanding and heading home. When he departed, I had the distinct feeling he would not be back.

A week passed and all is quiet. The sound of a new ice age, it seems, is silence. It's broken by the crack and thud of falling tree limbs, the howl and yap of prowling dogs abandoned by their caretakers, the whispering wind, the screaming wind and an occasional burst of gunshots.

Every episode of sound is an event that marks the passing of time. In the spaces between, I become aware of how dependent my sense of life was on the constant presence of sound: the hum of electricity, the drone of a refrigerator, the chatter of television, music on a radio, and the measured rhythm of traffic – even on a country road.

I've come to realize what silence means to me – or at least what it meant before the freeze: Silence is death.

This is a new breed of silence and it requires a new definition. How long will it be before I hear the heartbeat of nature, the song of the forest, the rhythmic balance of heaven and earth? How long will it be before I sense the force of my own being in a world that has always been indifferent? My whole life has been dependent on the perceptions of others – interpersonal relations, data transference, digital transactions, all the artificial creations of the mind, separate and distinct from the world in which I live.

This is not just an environmental catastrophe. It's an opportunity for self-discovery. It's a chance to find out who we are and why we exist. The meaning of life had long seemed an adolescent exercise, a ritual of aging, a futile pursuit, but now it seems the only pursuit worthwhile.

It's a world of constant wonder perpetually transforming itself from one set of rules to another, spawning revelation after revelation, none outliving the moment.

Survival is a powerful instinct. When it comes to the fore everything else subsides. Art and philosophy, defining forces in a civilized world, are confined to idle thought. Time ceases to function on an even continuum. Past and future recede as the moment is dominated by the need for food and shelter.

Dogs are gathering in packs. People are running short of food and letting their dogs fend for themselves. They roam the countryside, scavenging for scraps in garbage cans and dumps, fighting off rivals to protect territories, hunting for rabbits, squirrels, possums, raccoons and larger prey. The sound of a big kill fills the cold, silent air with horror for miles around.

Gunfire is becoming more frequent. Occasionally, the sound of shots is coupled with the yelp of a dog, telling a tale of the unspeakable and the unimaginable to come. People are now competing with their former companions on the hunt. How long will it be before the companion became the hunted?

I remember the story of the Donner Party – a tale of desperation and cannibalism – that sent shivers down my spine as a child. I wonder, gazing at my little dog Sadie, if it will come down to that final, dehumanizing act. Better to die. Better to die and be eaten than to live as a beast. Even a beast will not consume its own kind.

Nearly everyone in the country has dogs and guns. It is

not a comforting thought.

Taking stock of my supplies, it's not time to panic. With careful planning, I have enough canned goods to last the winter. Under a spell of paranoia, I buried half under the snow out back – just in case anyone came calling.

It's inevitable. When people run out of food they will come with open hands. They will come with guns. They will come with hungry children and grandparents.

What will I do when they come? How can I turn down a neighbor in need? If I welcome them, how much would they require? How many more would come? How long before there's nothing left?

I have not shot a gun since I was teenager. I shot a jay with a pellet gun and swore I would never shoot at a living thing again. I've kept that promise but now it seems the world has changed. I could not have envisioned a time when survival might depend on killing.

I begin to obsess on the sheriff's story of marauders. I make a plan. I bury all but a few cans of food. If intruders come, I'll head out the back and up the hill to a spot I cleared with a good view of the house and the road. They'll take the few cans of food and leave – or so I hope. If they don't, I'll fire a warning shot. If that doesn't work, I'll cover the chimney with a wet cloth and smoke them out.

It's my home and a man has a right to defend his home.

It's been snowing now for nine weeks without relief. Most of my time is spent keeping the fire going in the wood-burning stove. I have to maintain a clear path to the woodpile, find and dry a stock of kindling, select books to sacrifice page by page, keep the chute and chimney clear. It's a constant struggle but, without electricity, fire is critical for warmth, cooking and boiling water.

In my free time, I draw up contingency plans. What if the power never comes back? What if the storm never breaks? What if someone steals my food supply? What if the rescue teams never come?

RANDOM JACK

I was a city boy most of my life. I'm not well suited to survival in the wilderness. I can learn but the learning curve under these conditions is cruel. It always comes back to escape. I figure my best shot is to find a sled, harness the dogs and head south. Even if we die trying, it would be better than not trying at all.

I cannot believe that this frozen horror gripped the entire south. Somewhere the sun still shines, the snow melts and life returns to something resembling normal.

I'm taking my weekly bath, enjoying the liquid warmth while it lasts, when I hear the dogs bark. I know the difference between barking at deer or other dogs and barking to announce the arrival of humans.

Something about the best-laid plans races through my mind as I leap from the tub, pull on my jeans and race for the gun, crouching below the window. There's not enough time to dry myself, dress and climb the hill out back.

The barking intensifies and a series of images runs through my mind: the dogs circling, bearing their fangs, snapping, a man raising his gun, shooting, and pools of blood in the white snow. My dogs still panting, grasping for air, blood spilling on the snow, dying.

In one motion, I jump up, fling the door open, kneel, cock and fire. The dogs scatter and flee as a man throws up his hands and yells, "Don't shoot!"

He's an older man with a full, gray beard. Next to him, a woman huddled over two small children in a makeshift sled, their wide eyes peering out of layers of clothing. They're crying and the woman comforts them.

I stare at them in disbelief, lowering my rifle.

What has gone wrong with my mind? Had I come to this: Firing at unarmed people, at children, without even looking? This is supposed to be a time when people pull together, when the stronger are supposed to protect the weaker and when the able are supposed to help the needy.

Who am I? What have I become? An irrational and

frightened man so bent on protecting his territory that he would fire on a defenseless family.

They stare back at me, puzzled or pleading or both, until the man finally waves and they start moving down the road. I can hear the children's cries, muffled beneath their blankets, as the snow continues to fall.

"Wait!" I cry.

They stop and turn toward me, cautious and mystified, uncertain of the man who had fired at them only moments before.

"I'm sorry!" I yell. "Please, come on in!"

The dogs come back yapping and I call them inside, putting them in the study until they calm down. I welcome my visitors and excuse myself to get dried and dressed. When I emerge they're huddled around the woodstove, warm and comfortable.

"You gave us quite a fright," the man says.

"I'm sorry," I repeat. "I don't know what I was thinking."

"Well," says the woman, "I reckon we've all been out of sorts lately."

These are good country folk, strong, hard working and hard as nails, down to earth stock, unlikely to break even under the pressure of a Dixie freeze.

They sit on the sofa of the living room of my little house, gathering the children in their arms. It's a space that's comfortable for a man and his dogs but it's instantly cramped with the addition of visitors.

I feel the sting of second thoughts. This is my chance at salvation but I feel a knot in my gut. The sad truth is I couldn't stand to be with these people for more than a short evening in the real world – or rather, the old world, the world before the storm.

I listen to their story and it breaks my heart to think that it's the story of thousands just like them. They ran out of food. He ran out of bullets for his rifle and shot for his shotgun. They ran out of dry wood, candles and kerosene for their lantern. Then the chimney caught fire, burning furniture, and the roof caved in.

"One dern thing after another," he says, shaking his head in worry.

"The house next door is empty," I offer.

"Yes, sir," he replies. "It's all cleaned out. Ransacked. Windows and furniture all broke and scattered. We was up there before we come here. Surprised you didn't hear nothing."

Maybe I had. It's hard to tell. I hear a million sounds during the night, some real and some imagined.

"These children's hungry, mister," says the woman. "They's half froze."

She bows her head, as if she knows she's asking too much, and reaches for the hands of the children, a boy of five or six and his younger sister.

"They's our grandchildren," says the man. "They was visitin' when it all turned bad."

For the first time in so long I can hardly remember, I begin to see things from the eyes of another and it sobers me. I wonder what I would do in this man's position. I'm worried about my dogs. He's responsible for his grandchildren.

It occurs to me that my rifle is in the far corner of the room. The man and his family are between the gun and me.

I asked them to wait while I go outside to get food, half expecting the rifle to be pointed at me when I return. It's not. I hand over six cans of soup and vegetables and the woman goes to work in the kitchen.

I explain that there's probably enough food to last a few weeks if we're careful. I tell them I have a box of bullets for the rifle and enough wood to last out the winter. I let the dogs in and introduce them to the folks they had terrorized not a half hour before, explaining that they were in my care.

"I understand," says the man. "We had to let ours run,"

he says with genuine sorrow.

Just the same, I know it will become an issue if it ever comes down to the children or the dogs. It's a bridge we'll cross when we come to it.

They introduce themselves as the Coopers. The man is Perry, his wife Lily and the children Bobby and Tess. Lily empties the cans into a large pot, which she places on the woodstove to warm. Perry speaks of the latest news from the outside world. He had linked a shortwave radio to a car battery and tuned to an emergency broadcast out of Atlanta. The news is all bad.

"Remain calm," he relates. "The storm will break. It'll be over soon. But it ain't over. Ain't never going to be over. The Lord has come down upon the children of earth with a wrath of vengeance. Judgment day is upon us."

"Now, now, papa," says Lily, stirring the soup.

She passes out bowls and spoons and the Coopers eat in silence, except for the sound of smacking lips.

When they clean out their bowls, I ask how far south the storm goes. Perry hangs his head, takes a deep breath and leaves little room for hope.

"Snow in Macon, Birmingham, Montgomery. You got to get pert near the Gulf shore before it clears. But the roads blocked. They's no way out, mister. No way, no how."

"Well, now, papa," Lily replies in a soothing voice that comforts the children, "thanks to this young man, we got us a roof over our heads and a belly full of warm food. Don't sound like the wrath to me. Sounds like a blessing. Praise Jesus."

"Praise Jesus," the others echo.

She smiles and the warmth of her smile is passed from person to person until it seems even the dogs are smiling. I'm not much for the Jesus crowd but I decide then and there I would not mind spending my last days on earth, if it comes to that, with these gentle, kind-hearted people.

When night descends, I insist that Perry and Lily take the

bed and they reluctantly agree. I take the couch and the children lay out sleeping bags on the floor with the dogs. It's cozy and we all sleep soundly in the silent night. No dogs barking, no gunshots, no traffic, helicopters or airplanes, no electrical drone – only the soft, smoldering fire of the woodstove and dreams of faraway places where the sun still shines.

In the morning, I awaken to the sound of the children playing with the dogs. I sense something is different – even beyond the presence of visitors. I open my eyes and blink instinctively to shield myself from the bright light of the sun streaking through the window.

Bright, unfiltered sunshine for the first time in all these many weeks of snow, ice and bitter cold. I look outside and smile from head to toe. It's not snowing. In fact, the snow is visibly melting.

I'm about to wake the Coopers when the lights, the refrigerator, the television and radio, everything comes on at once. We gather in the living room and watch cheerful news people announce in perpetual cycles that the worst is over. The storm has lifted. Power is being restored.

"God bless," says Lily.

"God bless," say the children.

The nightmare of endless winter, of relentless white skies and fluttering snowflakes, is finally losing its icy grip and we are among the fortunate, the chosen and the blessed.

We survived.

HARD TIMES

When Izzy looked at Red at the far end of the bar, on the same barstool where she always sat, he knew she was the only one who could save him.

Times were hard. He didn't know whether the darkness sprang from within or without him. He didn't know whether the darkness within made the world seem a cruel and heartless place or a cruel and heartless world had darkened his vision. He knew only that it was draining him of his will to carry on. He had learned to turn his back on others when times were rough – a survival instinct. He didn't believe in self-sacrifice. He didn't believe in going down with the ship. Heroism was for suckers and today's heroes were tomorrow's martyrs. Now, however, when he needed a gentle voice, a softer landing, and a shoulder to lean on, there was no one to whom he could turn. He settled into a pattern of mindless repetitive behavior.

Every third Tuesday he boarded a city bus and negotiated his way to a downtown bank where he cashed his disability check. His status was a leftover from more liberal times. There was nothing physically wrong with him that a few months' abstinence and exercise would not cure. He had the constitution of an old Buick. No, his disability resided in his soul. He often wondered why he had not joined the army of huddled masses that crouched in doorways or sprawled on the sidewalk of Valencia Street in the Mission District where he tossed his hat. They must have lost his file in the shuffle.

Most every other day he rose at about the same time, showered, cooked and ate his only real meal of the day: scrambled eggs, bacon and toast. He would walk to the corner bar half a block from his one-room, second story apartment in a converted hotel from the forties. He sat on the same barstool, ordered a pitcher of beer, and drank until a regular came in and challenged him to a game of pool. His companions were a lot like him: they didn't say much and, when they did, they didn't say anything. He drank and played until late in the evening when he returned to his barstool and ordered a shot of whiskey.

He looked down to the far end of the bar and there she was, always in the same place, always with the same striking expression, her eyes turned down and inward. Everything she wore was of the vintage Gypsy mode, layers of shadow crowned by a blue velvet hat with a mother of pearl pin. She drank three dry martinis and she left up the back staircase without ever making contact with anyone in the bar except the bartender. And always, when he saw her, he had one more and savored it. Izzy could not move as long as Red was there. When she left, he left, and always, as he walked the pavement and climbed the stairs to the place he called home, he thought about her and he knew: She was the only one who could save him.

This had been Izzy's life for several months now. He knew from the bartender that her name was Maggie but she went by "Red" because of the waves of bright red hair she sported in her youth. She survived on a modest inheritance in a room upstairs from the bar. That was all he knew. Red never talked about her life. After a while no one asked.

Izzy thought about her all the time. He invented stories. Most of them were stories of heartbreak and misfortune, frustration and disappointment. There were some happy stories as well. Izzy was old enough to know that profound sorrow does not come to those who have not experienced profound joy. For Red, he invented a happy childhood.

She was an only child in a middle class, suburban setting. A doting father spoiled her. She had few wants and wishes that were not realized. She was a cheerleader and homecoming queen, engaged by the tender age of eighteen to be married to her high school sweetheart, the star quarterback of the football team. Something happened, however, between the dream and its consummation. Prince Charming went to college on a football scholarship while Red stayed home to pine and count the nights between holidays.

She discovered eventually that her prince had changed. A world of cold, cruel experience, a world of violence and injustice, a world of Vietnam protests, socialism and radical thought had come between the quarterback and his queen. Red was naïve but she did not lack intelligence or courage. She went out into the world to discover for herself what life beyond the white picket fence was like. What she discovered enlightened her and brought the budding beauty of her soul to bloom but not without a price. Her newfound idealism, absent the wisdom of experience, led her to misbegotten choices with tragic results.

Izzy could not bring himself to complete the story of Red's life. Often he tried but he could not define the moment or the sequence of events that cornered her in darkness. It was too intrusive. It was an invasion of the space that harbored her wounded soul. It was a place he could not go without her consent. He knew what he had to do. It was the only option left to him. It was his last hope.

"How are you?"

"Go away."

She looked up briefly and for the first time he saw the darkness in her eyes. He saw the light there as well, faint and obscure but familiar and warm. He sat down on the stool next to her. She did not raise her head.

"Are you deaf or stupid?"

"Stubborn," he replied. "I've been watching you."

"I know."

The silence between them was filled with tension and intrigue. It was not a silence of strangers. It was a silence of old friends separated by too much time and too many circumstances. It betrayed a realization that there was not enough light in the universe to bridge the darkness that kept them apart.

"I have a story," he said.

"Buy me a drink?"

"Sure."

"I'll listen to anyone's story as long as he buys me a drink and doesn't expect me to return the favor."

It was not true. Red was a fine looking woman despite her shroud. Many had offered and she always refused. Izzy was grateful for the opening and chose not to make an issue of it. He bought her a dry martini and told her the story, her story, the story of a quarterback and the American dream. When he got to the part where the story should have ended, he stopped and watched the silence between them grow lighter, less threatening and more inviting.

"You're not far off, mister," she said. "He wasn't the quarterback but he was a jock. I wasn't the homecoming queen but I was a lady in waiting. He went off to college and didn't come back. I went out into the world and it opened my eyes. End of story."

Of course, it was not the end of the story. Izzy could sense that she was calculating whether it was worth the telling. Would it drive him away and return her to the relative peace of isolation? Could she reveal herself to a stranger in a bar even if she secretly desired to? Izzy had come too far to let it rest. What remained of his life somehow depended on it.

"That's not the end, is it?"

She looked at him hard and cold. It was a look that had put off many a potential pickup but it did not have that effect on Izzy. He gave it back to her so that she knew he was a brethren spirit. It was no accident they had come together at this time and in this place.

"Buy me a drink?" she asked.

"Sure."

She waited until he made good on the promise. She sipped and examined him from head to tired shoes.

"You know the drill," she said. "You want to see mine, show me yours."

He smiled in appreciation of a dull wit.

"I have a confession," he said. "I know your story because it was mine. I *was* the quarterback. I was the local star who went off to college only to discover that I was just another kid on the block. When I finally made it home my prom queen was long gone. Everything was different. I was different. I went off to the Nam and became a body counter."

Izzy's hands began to shake and he lowered them to the bar. He swallowed his whiskey and ordered another.

"I counted bodies," he resumed. "I was lucky. I could type so I got a desk job. Counting dead bodies. I met a Vietnamese woman. You'd never guess where she was from. A little village called My Lai. When the war was over, she stayed. Counting bodies. I came home and became a cause chaser. I chased causes like a two-bit lawyer chases ambulances. I wanted to fill the space where my soul used to be. Political prisoners, save the salmon, offshore drilling, nuclear waste: wherever there was a protest, I was there. Eventually I ran out of causes. It's a young person's game. They could tell I was just a hanger on, not a true believer, and, when I saw it in their eyes, I couldn't do it anymore. I gave it up. That's how I came to be what I am today."

Red gave him a wink and a toast.

"Honest truth?" she asked.

"Best I can do."

"Fair enough."

She looked him over one more time just to be sure. Then she planted her eyes in her drink and began.

"You want to know what happened to me? Well, here goes. Straight up.

"I met a man. I know how stupid and how cliché that sounds: I met a man! But that's what happened. This man

118

was unlike any man I've ever known. He was brilliant, well spoken, attractive, and insightful. He had a great knowledge of the past and a vision for the future that answered every need and satisfied every desire. I loved that man in the purest way possible. I didn't want to possess him. I wanted to be with him. I believed in him. And I was not alone. He gathered us together and we became his following. When he decided to found his own society, not one of us hesitated. His name... was Jim Jones."

Izzy did not have to hear any more. Everyone in San Francisco knew the story by heart. Everyone from his generation knew someone who died in the Jonestown massacre. It was Hale-Bopp squared and it was before anything like that had ever happened. Jonestown, more than Kent State, Martin Luther King and Bobby Kennedy, was an end to an era of hope. It was a dagger to the heart of anyone who ever dared to dream of an enlightened world.

"I'm sorry," he said.

He wiped away a tear and saw that Red was doing the same. They were indeed brethren spirits. They were a strange kind of soul mates, whose tears were composed of the same blood, the same sweat and heartbreak. He motioned to a nearby table and affected sober bravado.

"Care to join me for a nightcap?"

"Sure, mister," she smiled. "One more for the road."

It was the first time either of them had abandoned their stations at the bar.

THE HOLE

Morgan hiked long enough to lose track of the days. He carried as little as possible of anything that would remind him of other human beings: No machines, no devices with moving parts, no books, no words or photographs. He carefully removed labels from his clothing and printed matter from his packages of dried fruit and jerky. He considered going native style, buckskin and pouches made from the scrotums of mammals, but he decided it was missing the point. He did not reject society. He was only escaping the pervasive and endless maze of its influence.

He approached his goal on the seventh day of hiking. He did not see any signs of human presence. No wrappers or aluminum cans, no smoke in the distance, no shoveled under fire pits. More importantly, for three consecutive nights (he slept only a few hours each night), his dreams had been free of human presence. In fact, they seemed to have shed their earthly hold altogether. No longer bound by the force of gravity, he floated in a sea of pure energy, absorbing sensations, observing patterns of light, shadow and dancing colors, drifting within and without miraculous realms without physical presence, presence without being, forms without structure – an entire universe with completely unfamiliar rules. It was what he had longed for and what had always seemed unattainable until now.

No one knew his whereabouts. As much as a year would pass before anyone even noticed his absence. He had a rambling lifestyle. Not even his family and closest friends could count on seeing him or hearing from him for months at a time. After six months they would begin to wonder. A few phone calls would be placed but there would be no way of tracking him down. Another six months and they would finally gather to commemorate his passing.

There would be music, dance and renewed friendships. Stories would be shared over the flames of a great bonfire. More than a few tears would be shed. They would grieve and praise him for the many vicarious adventures that enriched their lives. But, alas, Morgan would not be dead – only sleeping, dreaming, exploring the deep inner spaces, drifting in the great void beyond the beyond.

He told no one his plans. No one was capable of truly understanding. Some of them were capable of intellectual understanding. They were artists who confronted the same dilemma: Art in a media age. No one could escape the maze. Even the most radical of the avant-garde struggled to produce an original concept. In the constant effort to find an audience an artist had to tap the aesthetic mode of the day. Rejecting the audience was old news and a loser's game. There was no way around it.

His friends and family would empathize with their comrade in creativity but in the end, even they would label his endeavor insane and, fearing the karmic balance, they would feel compelled to stop him by any means.

Suicide is a nasty word. It was not suicide. It was an affirmation, a confirmation, a celebration of art itself and the creative instinct, of everything he cherished and relentlessly pursued throughout his life. If he failed, however, it would be perceived as suicide and that was the point. He could no longer exist in a world so dominated by the perception of his peers. Everything he had ever done, written, sculpted, painted, photographed or performed had been shaped by the expectations, the demands, the criticisms, the praise, the relentless and pervasive observations of others.

Could true art exist in such a world? Could the artist survive in an environment so flooded with media distortion? Why else had so many artists historically chosen to alter their senses and perceptions with hallucinogens, depressants, anti-depressants, boosters, poppers, uppers, downers, injected, inhaled or otherwise consumed?

It was no longer so simple and easy. The electronic age had saturated human consciousness. It was reported that some had begun to dream in short, three-second sound bites and MTV style clips. There was no ready remedy for this ailment. The machine had become the man. The mind of man had become the machine.

Morgan sat down beside a brisk, narrow waterfall to bathe his aching limbs and gather his thoughts. These mountains were full of chasms and caves suitable to his adventure, his experiment, his sacred journey into the nether land of dreams. As he scanned the surroundings, an overhang caught his eye.

There! That's the place! It was a strange and exhilarating sensation. He was inspired and compelled by the feeling that each step carried him to his destiny. Not unlike John Glenn or Alan Shepard, Picasso or Andy Warhol, he was propelled by the conviction that he was somehow making history. The uplift carried a down draft as well. It was a heavy burden to bear the torch that would become a responsibility to those that followed. He vowed that he would not succumb to a sudden resurgence of doubt and timidity, the cowardice of his native soul.

He visually marked the overhang against its surrounding landmarks and filed it in his mind. It would take several hours to reach it and several more to prepare.

In fact, the preparations began long before the decision had been made. He had given the better part of a year to the project he christened "Daedalus" in reference to the Athenian who constructed the Labyrinth of the Minotaur in Greek mythology. Only Daedalus possessed the knowledge and the key to negotiate the maze and return.

He spent much of his time researching the herbs and elixirs he required. He gathered the ingredients from their natural habitats – belladonna, mug wart, citronella, birch, pyrethrum, wolfs bane, larkspur, pennyroyal and nasturtium – for a concoction he would spread over his body to keep rodents, insects and snakes from feeding on his sleeping flesh. He gathered mandrake, wormwood, primrose, chamomile, passionflower, opiate and Yerba Buena for a sleeping potion that would ease him into the nether land.

His experiments in mixtures and dosages had brought him to the edge of excess. More than once he had to use powerful emetics and purgatives to expel the potion from his body. At length, he arrived at a solution that enabled him to sleep for three weeks at a time. It was enough. He would sleep for three weeks, awaken, attend to his nutritional needs, and refill the water pouch (attached to a thin reed, fastened to his teeth, so that it slowly dripped into his mouth, triggering a swallow reflex that would provide a constant supply without awakening him). He would then ingest another dosage of the sleeping potion.

The cycle would be repeated nine times for a total of twenty-seven weeks. He would then return to the civilized world with a message from the beyond. He would possess a mind cleansed of social influence. He would hold the seeds for the first truly original creation in the technological, media-dominated age. He would immerse himself in art and emerge with a body of work that would revolutionize the core meaning of art itself. He would turn the world on its head.

He proceeded slowly, deliberately, climbing the last mountain and savoring the moment, as if recording each step for posterity. History drove him now. It was his mentor and guide and it would be his benefactor. No longer would he have to hustle for a gig at a local performance hall, begging for shows at storefront galleries, groveling for a share of the pitiful arts endowment, reworking his creations to suit popular trends or social acceptability. He would become the Guru of the Garde, the Big Daddy of Dada, the Kat of Kool, the Big Banana Cheese Wiz of the Bonzo crowd, the Shaman's Shaman of the Gohonzo crowd, the Baddest of the Bad and the Diggest of the Dig. Morgan smiled at the prospect but refused to revel. He began his mantra as he neared the precipice:

Free yourself of thought, free yourself of feeling, free yourself of words, free yourself of senses...

Atop the mountain of destiny, he stood for a moment in perfect stillness to gaze out at a magnificent panorama of granite, pine and Parish blue skies streaked with delicate wisps of white clouds. It was perfection and he breathed it in. It would be his last appreciation of the great mother's beauty before he climbed into the void. He wanted to absorb the essence of her raw and natural grace. It was so simple yet so beyond our grasp. If a key existed on heaven or earth, he would find it.

It was as he envisioned, less a cave than a hole. It was sheltered by huge, overlapping granite walls, tightly fitted, allowing no light. It was cool and relatively comfortable. The contour of its solid rock floor would provide drainage and there was only one way in.

He lit a candle, fashioned a bed, and screened the entrance with pine boughs adorned with his repellant brew. Stripped to a loincloth, he spread his concoction thickly over his body, carefully about the eyes, nose and mouth. He drew a protective circle and sat cross-legged, placing his vials of potion and sacred objects before him: owl feather, crystal, bundle of sage, mother of pearl, onyx, a guitar pick. He brewed a tea of lemon, sage and spearmint on a Bunsen burner to counteract the potion's repulsive taste, poured and stirred the potion, and said a prayer for the occasion:

"Great Spirit, godhead, master of all things, center of all being, force of all in one, bless this adventure and guide me in wisdom as I am guided by faith. In purity of heart and soul, I give myself to this destiny. Amen."

He drank the portent brew, lay down and closed his eyes.

The effect was instantaneous. He surrendered all thought or thought surrendered him. He let go and instantly found himself in a realm beyond the senses, an undiscovered land of awe: dancing bundles of light in a liquid sky. He was floating in the cosmic sea, weightless, timeless, and free of all constraint. His awareness slipped from his conscious being, leaving him reeling ever faster toward the black hole of infinite mystery. Already the word surrendered. Language was no longer useful. Knowledge threw up its hands in humility and wept.

Take a thousand points of light and place them on the head of a pin; multiply each by a thousand and a thousand again. A light so brilliant it transforms vision and melds all that is known to all that is imagined combined with all that is beyond imagining into one glorious truth. After all his years of struggle and experimentation, risk and challenge, prayer and frustration, Morgan was home at last. Home. In the hole...

When he awakened he knew something was wrong. He had returned too rapidly to his physical being. Startled and disoriented, he became aware of dryness in his mouth, a burning in his throat and a sickening in his gut. He felt his body being pressed to the granite floor and he recognized the symptoms: Belladonna poisoning.

How could it have happened? Something about the best-laid plans rambled through his shattering mind. He managed to smile at the irony of his situation. Only in death can you escape the circumstances of life. Was it suicide after all? Somewhere in the deep hole of his psyche, had he known all along that this would be the end – his final dance of destiny?

If his body were ever found it would certainly be pronounced suicide. The presence of Belladonna would leave no doubt. But those who knew him best would take it for what it was: the last glorious act of an artist in search of perfect expression, a celebration of the creative soul, and a tribute to the adventurous spirit of a man who never lost hope.

He closed his eyes, breathed his last measured breaths, relaxed and let go. He left behind all his plans, all his dreams, all his thoughts and desires, all his memories and cares. He let go of life and enjoyed the ride.

FIVE OF SEVEN

Standing on the deck, overlooking a cold winter Pacific, I counted the waves and as I counted I considered the stages of human life on earth. Shakespeare counted seven, from the mewling infant to second childhood and the grave, but I had an affinity for reinventing the wheel. I quickly scanned through the early stages:

Infancy – when the individual is submerged and lost in the surrounding world,

Childhood – when the individual is the center of all being,

Adolescence – when libidinal hormones dominate and so obscure the individual, and

Young Adulthood – when the individual realizes he is both a part of the world and apart from the world.

The fourth stage was the time of hope. A brief window of opportunity opens, making real change possible. I reflected that it was a time when jeans wore out at the knees. Later they would wear out at the seat. It is a time of doing, of acting, of being, and not of reflection. It is a period most of us cling to when our discontented psyches require comfort.

I breathed in and savored a nostalgic moment, a remembrance of how things were, the salve of a lost generation. I was beyond the fourth stage. I could no longer deny it. I had already fought and lost that battle. There is nothing more pathetic than a middle-aged man pretending to be young.

Middle Age – when the individual accepts the futility of his life.

The midlife crisis to the middle-aged is as acne to the

adolescent. It is a time when we discover the deterioration of the body.   We awaken one day to find a belt of fat surrounding our midriff and we soon realize we are dying. Our greatest fear is not death so much as dying in discomfort and obscurity, alone. Those who respond in denial act out inane scenarios of radical change, calculated to set back the clock, and failing with the dull thud of the obvious. Those who accept the change generally become passive, limiting our involvement to rhetorical grumblings of discontent between bottles of beer or glasses of wine.

I was definitively in the fifth stage. Five of seven. Not a whole lot of life left. Not a whole lot of mortal coil to be unwound. I hoped the sixth stage would be that of the elder, respected for his wisdom and truth, but I realized that the respected elder was often omitted in contemporary life. The seventh stage, of course, is death and that part of life that is dying.

I was not ready to think about death and dying though I thought about it all the time. I preferred to think about change. I was thinking now about recapturing the fire of youth, the spark of yearning and desire, and wondering if it was possible without falling into the predictable pattern of midlife folly. Try as I might, I could not think of a single example where it had been done. I pulled out a cigarette and decided to watch television, an activity that would consume the day without requiring the engagement of my mind. I needed my mind and I was afraid of losing it.

The phone rang. I considered not answering it – my standard mode of indifference – but something about my train of thought required me to act. I needed to be a participant in life rather than an onlooker.

"Hey, Jake! It's Buzz."

Jake was my first name but Buzz, outside my immediate family, was the only one to use it. Everyone else knew me as Harrison. Buzz was an adventurer. If anyone could drag a person out of the deepening hole that was currently swallowing me, it was Buzz Henshaw. I had not seen him for more than a year. That was Buzz. In his mid thirties, his spirit was forever young and he was always on the move. In the metaphor of seven stages, Buzz was stuck in the fourth and I envied him.

"Where the hell are you?"

"Just down the road. Thought I'd shout out a warning before I show up at your door."

Buzz was on a perpetual crusade to light a fire in the lives of those he knew. He hated the ruts that people settled into. He despised the scenarios of revolving melodrama that most people call life. If Buzz is in town, you brace yourself for a shakeup. This time I'm ready for it. In fact, I'm desperate for it.

By the time he pulls into the driveway in his old, beat up Dodge van, the word "yes" is perched on my lips. If Buzz is primed to make a World Tour on pocket change, I'm prepared to drop everything and move. With Buzz nearly anything is possible. Still, I'm a little surprised to see that Buzz is not alone. It's not unusual for him to be traveling with a woman. He might have encountered her yesterday or they might have been together for months. With Buzz it doesn't matter. He regards every individual he encounters as if they're long lost friends.

Something about this woman, however, is different. They move in harmony and keep one eye on the other even as they approach my door. They hold to each other as if they possess a sacred trust.

"This is my wife, Angie," says Buzz with a grin.

We embrace amidst nervous laughter and shuffling feet. It's cold outside so we headed in to a warm fire without the usual small talk. I go to hustle up some coffee and try to discard the disorientation in my gut. Buzz is the last man on earth I expected to get married. Marriage is a legal contract, a financial agreement that guarantees resentment once the relationship ends as it almost always does. But here he stands, smiling like a proud father, feeling no need to explain himself.

Buzz follows me into the kitchen to help with the coffee.

"Is everything alright?" he asks.

He had an ability to size up a situation in an instant. He developed the talent in his years on the road where survival depends on the ability to skirt danger by recognizing it in advance.

I shake my head. There's no point in trying to hide my disappointment. I was born with the kind of face and expressions that render me incapable of deception.

"I can't believe you're married," I confess.

"What else?"

"I was hoping you were here to rescue me. I'm stuck. I'm bored. I was hoping you were going to propose some great adventure."

Buzz laughs as he delivers coffee to his waiting wife. He stands behind her, rubbing her shoulders. Angie is a sixties woman with long, braided hair and layers of flowing clothes. She's a mixture of new age wisdom and down home practicality. She has a soulful spirit, contemplative, sympathetic and undisturbed by the conflict unfolding before her. She's exactly what Buzz needs to plant his feet on the earth while his mind explores the stars.

"What we have in mind," says Buzz, "*is* an adventure. It's just not the kind of adventure you expected."

"Let's hear it," I say. I did not intend my words to strike with the impact I observe on both their faces. I'm being terse. I'm treating a brother and his wife with the thoughtless regard one would have for a traveling salesman.

"It can wait," replies Buzz.

It so often happens that the poisons we spit out come back in triplicate. I feel like a salted slug, disintegrating in my own stew. I apologize but the best we can do is to agree to let it rest a while. Angie suggests we go down to the beach and build a bonfire. I grab some blankets and a bottle of brandy and off we go.

As we sit huddled in blankets, gazing into the fire through smoke and mist, we begin the ritual of story telling that traditionally secures the bonds of friendship and affection.

Angie begins with a tale of romance. It seems she's a Renaissance woman whose parents are financially secure and supportive enough to put her through four years of a liberal arts education at the University of Colorado. When she graduated, she opted to stay rather than return to her Indiana roots. It was there, on the streets of Boulder, that she first encountered Buzz. She's a writer, a dancer and piano player. Buzz is the finest improvisational flautist never to walk on stage at Lincoln Center. Instinctively, she began dancing to his improvisational muse. It was love at first riff.

Buzz takes over from there. They went back home to visit family and friends in Alabama. There was an encounter with the ghost of WC Handy. They received the blessings of a voodoo queen in New Orleans. There were brushes with the law and close encounters in biker bars. From Atlanta to New York to Chicago, there was a series of gigs and happenings. They committed high crimes and misdemeanors against the artistic establishment. On the westward push, they visited the Burning Man Festival and had a conversation with Don Juan on their private journey to Ixtlan. There was a cleansing ceremony on the Navaho reservation and a moonlit night at Grand Canyon. They saw the Crazy Horse monument in the Black Hills and the memorial at Wounded Knee. They got married in Reno and headed north to visit an old friend on the Oregon coast.

If it were anyone but Buzz, I would not have believed half of it. He was a collector of stories but not an embellisher. I was reminded of our rabblerousing days in the Haight. I was always more or less the quiet one. Buzz was the spirit of the beat, the soul of rebellion, a leader of leaders and the envy of every artist who crossed his path. He was

Jack Cassidy and Coleman Hawkins. He was Mario Salvo and Jackson Pollock. He was the heart of a revolution that did not die when Nixon ended the war. Everything that was good and sacred lives on in the adventures of Buzz Henshaw. It could never die as long as Buzz carried on.

I settle into a reflective mood, longing for far away times and places I never knew, experiences I never had, faces I never had the pleasure of seeing, and adventures I only dreamed of having. I yearn for the memories of the man who sits before me. I wonder if he knows how much his friends depend on him to bring his stories to their tables. I can see by the look in his eyes, he knows and understands.

My story is short. It's two years after my divorce and nothing has changed. I'm still active in the local art scene. I had a few shows and tried my hand at performance art. I'm a little fish in a little pond with little hope of finding my way out.

There's an awkward moment of silence before we settle into the familiar pattern of reminiscence, anecdotes and social commentaries between pokes at the fire. The sky is clear and the sun is about to turn our world into a majestic wonderland when Angie suggests we spend the night on the beach. I run up to the house for sleeping bags and a bucket of chicken. On a whim, I grab a seven iron and three golf balls.

"Remember the Zen Golf Tour?" I ask.

It's a rhetorical question. Buzz and I wrote the book of Zen Golf. The highlight of the journey was two sacred shots into the infinite void of the Grand Canyon under a full moon on a mystic summer night. We spoke of hitting shots into both oceans that summer but we never made it. It was time to fulfill half the promise.

I tee my ball on a mound of sand as the sun first strikes Pacific waters in an explosion of burning, bright orange and yellow light.

"This one is for the journey. May it never end."

Buzz tees up and says, "This is to new beginnings."

Angie follows with: "This is to friendship and the journey within."

We sit back and let the moment speak for itself. We have come to a deeper understanding than we might have reached in a month of exchanging stories and anecdotes. It's all on the table.

Buzz pulls out a penny whistle and scores the sunset with music that springs from the earth, soars to the heavens and returns home in serenity. I realize what to do. I remember a night at the end of a long stretch of highway. We were high and drunk with fatigue. Buzz said something he had never said before: He did not know how long he could keep going.

We crashed in a sleazy roadside motel and there, beneath blinking neon lights with tin jazz on a bedside radio, he confessed that he envied me. He envied anyone who could stay in one place and keep the dream alive. He had a dream he stored in the back of his mind, waiting for the day it would welcome him. He wanted to start a little jazz and poetry café – a place people could come, day or night, hear some music, poetry or muse. It would be a place of comfort, a home for dreams and weary adventurers.

I sleep well. We all do. In the morning, back at the house over coffee, I tell them what I want to do. I hand over the keys to my house and car. I give them my ATM card and the secret code. Everything I have is theirs.

"In exchange I want that old van, a penny whistle, and a promise that I'll always be welcome at your door."

There are the usual protests but that soon passes. We have come to an understanding. It's time for me to live the life I dream. It's my turn to carry the torch. It's what my soul, my spirit and my inner self requires.

Call it a midlife crisis if you will. For me, it's the only choice I could make. It does not matter what anyone thinks. It does not even matter what I think or what I would think when I pass into an older and wiser stage. I got the shot and I took it. Simple. Clear. Clean.

There is no feeling on earth more genuine and true than an open road and a heart full of adventure – unless of course it is to be home with the one you love.

THE SWEAT, THE CLUB & THE ROAD

I. The Ritual.

The ritual begins with a quiet meditation, relaxation, a cleansing of consciousness, clearing the path for a flow of imagery like ancient memories from the universal mind. I imagine the tribes of the northern plains centuries ago, before the white man decided to claim the continent as his own. I conjure the Lakota, Cheyenne, Shoshone and Crow. I summon Big Foot at Wounded Knee. I picture the Sun Dance, warriors strung to the tree of life, dancing beyond pain in sweat and blood. I contemplate the seven rites of White Buffalo Woman. I summon Wavoka, founder of the Ghost Dance, and Crazy Horse, the Strange Man of the Oglala.

I don the sacred robes and dance. I join the fire circle and sing the sacred songs. I hear the prophecies and watch them unfold. I sit with Don Juan and ingest the sacred seed. I share the peyote vision of a desert landscape. I ride the lost highway west. The west is the best.

II. The Sign.

Somewhere in the great expanse of the Arizona desert there is a short stretch of pavement labeled Route 666. It was there, in the summer of love, that I caught a ride with three hell bent losers on a road to nowhere. The desolation, the scattered sage brush and drifts of sand, the unforgiving sun, the smell of gasoline, the sign of the scorpion on a dead man's grave, the sense that even the coyote trickster had abandoned the place, was an image etched in my mind alongside Dante's seven circles of hell.

III. The Cleansing.

I burn sage and drink herbal tea – the cleansing before the cleansing. I look into the eyes of the crow at Grand Canyon. I clothe myself in layers – the robes before disrobing. I regard each moment with mindfulness – Zen. I am aware of the kinesthetic sensation of thought. I am aware of every sound, from the distant roving coyote to the shifting of wood on its foundation of concrete. I am aware of every particle within my field of consciousness. I am aware of the spirits within and without. Mitakuye Oyasin. All my relations.

The Sweat is an opportunity that does not present itself every day. In the everyday life of an ordinary man, it does not present itself at all. It is the most basic of all sacred rituals. It is the cleansing before the Sun Dance. It is the cleansing before vision quest, before the healing ceremony, and before the keeping of a soul. It is not to be taken lightly.

IV. Rules of the Road.

The wise hitchhiker does not take every ride he is offered. He selects a ride as a tourist might choose a restaurant. He sizes up the risk at a glance. He does not carry a sign with a city of destination. It would not allow an out. If he uses a sign it contains a road and a direction (Route 66 West) or a state (CA or Bust!) but not a city. When a car stops he is first to inquire, "Where are you headed?"

Once he sizes up the situation, he calculates the risk versus the reward. He maintains his options. It's all about protecting options. If the ride says he is bound for Tuba City and you don't like his looks, you say your mind is set on Santa Fe. You thank him and add, "I've been stuck in Tuba

City before." This informs him you know the rules.

If he changes his story, you thank your guardian spirits and walk away. Now he knows you are on to him. He has no way of knowing if you have a knife or a gun but he has already figured it out: You're more trouble than you're worth. In the final calculation, this is what protects you.

V. The Bus Stop.

"Where you headed, friend?"

I am sitting in a bus station in Flagstaff, Arizona, trying to stay awake until my bus arrives. My eyes droop and my head drops periodically like a stone from an open hand, snapping back into a waking world of concrete floors and plastic chairs with televisions attached to them. A woman catches me just as I am about to nod off. I snap back to a reality of instinct where survival is king.

"North," I reply.

She laughs. She knows the code. She is a leathered goddess in a realm of normality. No one takes the bus any more but soldiers and the poor. No knock. It's just the way it is. She's definitely not a soldier so I figure she's poor. Probably an addict. I size her up the way she has sized me up for the last few minutes. I figure she has an angle. She wants more than idle conversation.

"Can you be a little more specific?" She laughs.

I realize I am not on the road anymore so there's no real need to protect my options.

"Denver," I reply.

In truth, my destination is Boulder. I don't know why I say Denver except you never know how twenty miles of error might come into play.

"Why Denver?" she asks.

"I know some people there."

It's an honest answer (within twenty miles of the truth) and it figures in the equation. I want to go where someone knows my name. I want to be where someone smiles at a familiar face and invites me to dinner to talk about old times. But the real reason is: I was once enchanted by a dancer there. I am the kind of guy who remembers things like that. In hard times, such as these, my memories pull me back as if it were possible to recapture the ragged glory of yesteryear.

"Looks like we've both got a long wait," she says, glancing at the schedule of departures. "There's a club down the road. Want to come?"

A quick scan and I can think of no reason to decline until my chin bounces off my chest mid thought.

"I've got something to pick you up," she says. She flashes a vial with an inhaler attached and my mind is made up for me. For the first time, I notice she is attractive. Maybe not pretty but the kind of woman who grabs your eye and holds it on demand.

So I find myself dancing with a leathered goddess in a sea of raving punk rockers on drugs in Flagstaff, Arizona. Who would have imagined? The sweat is pouring down our bodies like a waterfall. With every move, it splashes in glitters of flashing light. I am enraptured by sweat in glittering light and I realize I am in the middle of some kind of ritual. It is a ritual of sweat.

VI. The Sweat.

The old one says: Once we begin we cannot go back.

We are a circle of twelve mostly white, mostly yuppie types and he is telling us it is time to decide. The Sweat is not to be taken lightly. It is a sacred rite. It opens the door to the spiritual realm. It invokes the powers. As with all rituals, the powers can do good or harm depending on the contents of the heart and the intentions of the participants.

"Do not take this step for the wrong reasons," he says. "Do not do this thing if you are afraid."

The old one is the real deal. He is a Lakota spirit guide

from the Pine Ridge reservation. He takes these gigs for two hundred dollars and expenses but he does not take them lightly. He will use the money to help his people. It's a reasonable compromise though there are many within his own community that would accuse him of betrayal. He speaks softly but his words drop like stones into the well of ancient knowledge.

A bearded man, who is our host and leader by right of property, strikes a pose and speaks for us in a voice that is not quite his own: We are ready.

While we awaited the arrival of our guide, he spoke of the old ways as if he were a genuine sage. He brings up the Lakota phrase that translates to: All my relations. Having studied the ways of the Lakota, I am eager to show my colors. "Mitakuye Oyasin," I say, pronouncing every sound and syllable phonetically. It is a term I have only seen in print.

The bearded man looks at me with awkward disapproval. He believes somehow that I have challenged his leadership. He wants to count coup. He corrects my pronunciation.

I knew then I was right about the bearded man: He's a bad ride.

VII. The Bad Ride.

"You oughta take that bandana off," the driver says.

Why do these guys always have bad teeth?

"Yeah," says his companion. "Someone might mistake you for an Indian."

I am a fool. Until this moment, it never occurred to me that being mistaken for an Indian is a bad thing. I take the bandana off. It's a rule of the road: Accept the hand you are dealt. Never rock the boat.

I ride on the driver's side in the back seat of an old Chrysler with three Wild West cowboys and by now I know it was a bad choice. Looking back, I probably knew it from scratch but seven hours on desolation row does strange things to one's powers of observation. They pump me about how much money I have and are just smart enough to figure out I don't have much. So they let me in on their plan to knock over a gas station. They want to know: "Are you in?"

I tell them I have to think about it. It would not be wise to decline straight up. They would take it as an insult. I don't agree either because, once you are in there is no turning back. So I bide my time and calculate the risks of jumping from a moving vehicle.

VIII. The Kiss.

"Not bad," she says with a smile, as our lips part in a sea of pounding sound and glittering sweat.

Moments before, she had stopped dancing and pressed her body against mine. She waited for our eyes to lock so I could see the purity and innocence of her intentions. She pulled my lips to hers and swallowed my resistance. On the walk back to the bus station, she tells me the story of a woman who's down on her luck. It's a common story about an abusive relationship and the absence of a way out.

I want to be empathetic. As a conscious member of the human race, how can I turn my back on a sister in need? But my survival instincts are strong. How can I carry the burden of a fellow traveler when it's hard enough to carry my own?

She kisses me again and the sweet intoxication of her tongue on mine revives my better instincts. I hear the voice of a guardian angel from an old David Lynch movie:

Don't turn your back on love, pilgrim.
Don't turn your back on love.

IX. Last Chance.

"Last chance," says the driver as we pull into an old

Mobil Oil station about a mile off the highway. "If you're with us, boy, now's the time."

I wait for the car to come to a complete stop. I get out and walk away. I do not look back. The cowboys have a gun but it is old and rusty – more for show than firing. They won't waste a shot on me. I'm not worth the trouble. Anyway, they have a job to do. It may not be much of a job but it is the only job they have. They too are the unfortunate ones. They are the products of bad choices. It is what it is.

On the walk back to the highway I find myself wishing them well, hoping they will not be killed, and grateful they didn't kill me. I'm allowed to carry on. I will not be held accountable today.

I hear sirens as I wait alongside the road. It's their day to pay. I catch a ride from someone's mother who looks at me as if I'm her lost son. She takes me straight to the bus station and hands me a fifty-dollar bill. I want to advise her to be careful picking up hitchhikers but I see she has no fear. She has a way with people. She takes care of herself. Somewhere in the back of my mind, I sense that she's right: Saints and angels have no fear.

X. All My Relations.

The old one smokes us with sage as we enter the lodge and move to our places around the pit. Large round red-hot stones are transported from the fire outside and placed in the pit. The entrance is sealed and the old one says a prayer in his native tongue. The bearded man dips a ladle into the water bucket and pours it on the stones. Steam explodes in the darkness and the cloud envelops us.

We are asked to contemplate our ancestors, our brothers and sisters, the four-legs, the six and the eight. We are asked to remember our mother earth, the water, the fire and the air. The old one speaks of the oneness of all beings, the sanctity of things upon the planet.

We experience the Sweat in four stages, each time cycling out into the crisp night air and back into the lodge again. More stones are added, more water poured, more steam and heat, more than I could have imagined and still endured. The stones that were once red with heat turn white and faces of the ancients are clearly drawn in them. The story of the earth is told in pictures that form within the sacred steam, now clearly visible in the pitch-black of the lodge.

I begin to experience all the events of my own life as if they occurred simultaneously. I begin to understand that all things, however distant, contribute to this moment of near perfection, bliss and atonement. I let go the shame, the pride, the blame and the sorrows of my soul. I understand now. I understand that everyone, great and small, plays a part in the great mystery. I forgive us our ignorance. I forgive the highway cowboys. I forgive the punk rockers on dope. I forgive the bearded man his jealousy. I forgive myself. I bless all beings as I bless myself. Suddenly there is peace.

It took us thousands of years to lose faith in our fellow beings. It may take as long to regain it. Still, in a moment of clarity, forgiveness is a beginning.

I reach for the hand of my leather goddess and find it waiting. We walk out into the clear skies of a moonlit night. The wonder and the beauty and the joy walk with us.

"Mitakuye Oyasin," I say to the old one.
He smiles but he does not correct me.

THE NAKED ABYSS

Vera! Vera! What has become of you?
Does anybody else in here feel the way I do?

Pity the poor man who dies without a name on some forgotten street corner. He was some mother's son. He was the hope, the dream and the smile in his father's eyes.

There was a time in life as in art and literature when civilization thrived on heroes. They were individuals ordinary and extraordinary that overcame hardship to do great good in the world. Through the tradition of story telling we lived their lives vicariously. We sought to be like them. We borrowed their strength and fortitude. We became better than ourselves by reaching beyond our self-defined limits.

Today we idolize so many people for so many reasons that we have reduced the concept of heroism to celebrity. The legacy of heroism gave way to Andy Warhol's theory of fifteen-minute fame.

When he was only three he had bright eyes and great ambitions. He was going to make his parents proud. When he was five, he was going to show them all. They were wrong. He was going to be somebody. He was going to save lives. He was going to be a hero. He was going to be a star. When he was seven, he was going to start a band. When he was nine, he was going to join a gang. When he was thirteen he chased his dreams in the land of liquid horizons. When he was seventeen he was going to set the world on fire. When he was twenty-three he did. When he was twenty-seven he shot a man for twenty bucks. When he was thirty he looked fifty. When he was thirty-six he was lying in a pool of blood, his dreams fading, his hopes gone, his view of the world a gutter and his future over the rainbow.

We let him down. He let himself down. He fell for it. He bought into a system that counted him out before he could discover a larger universe. We will not mourn for him. We will let him pass into the endless night, the naked abyss that awaits us all. We will not reach for him for he would pull us down with a smile of sarcasm. In his dying breath, he only wants revenge.

Vera! Vera! What has become of you?

She became a topless dancer in a jazz club in the lower ninth ward until the inevitable day when her appeal no longer paid the bills. A spiral downward to a trailer park with overgrown weeds and a black market economy. She gasped her last breath faking orgasm with a bald man when a homegrown meth lab kissed the heavens goodbye.

He was driving down Highway 66 heading west from a pilgrimage to the sacred Chiricahua Mountains, where the face of Cochise gazes at the heavens, when he chanced upon an offshoot reading Route 666. He turned around and went back the way he came. There are odds no gambler should take. He ended up at a dreary motel with a bar across the street. He asked for number nine but it was in repair. He asked for thirteen and she tossed him the key. He stayed for two weeks, drinking, eating salted snacks and waiting for something to happen.

She opened the door and asked him if he wanted a job. He already had one but how could he turn her down? She had dark eyes that sucked him in. They spent three days having hot, trailer park sex, doggie style, down and dirty, drug induced; he never saw it coming.

She drew a map and googled it just to make sure. She told him to meet her at the mark, seven o'clock sharp. Sure he said and drove to the next town.

These kinds of things never happened to him so he was sure it was happening to someone else, someone he could not trust. He picked up a hitchhiker outside of Tucson and began peppering her with questions. She was on the run. A broken family, an old story, a brutal relationship and a bagful of pills: She asked if he wanted to try something and he said why not, he was going nowhere. They grabbed a six-pack at a local market and drove deep into the desert on a gallon of gas. He made his move but she showed no interest so they popped a few pills and let the barren earth swallow them.

Time cranked to a quivering halt, insects swirling, heat coming in waves, night riding in on a yellow moon and a blue-bellied lizard settled on his nose. The lizard gave him knowledge as they wandered the moonlit night, picking flowers and collecting the seeds of perception.

She placed them in a leather bag tied round her waist. She was building a new life, seed by seed, and he was her appointed guide. A dozen more and they could start their own cult. A dozen years and they could found their own religion. How can you start a religion he wondered without sex? She folded him in her sprawling limbs and collected the seeds of creation.

He awakened on a broad flat rock, his clothes neatly folded, the sun bearing down on his reddened body. The woman was gone. The car was nowhere. He pulled on his jeans, his shirt, tied his undershirt around his head and began walking. An hour later he found her sleeping in his car: out of gas. He told her to find another ride and walked ten miles with a gas can. She waited at the car. He came back in a pickup with a kid in his twenties, buckteeth and smiling. She was down to accessories: black panties and a maroon bra. She asked for a ride and the kid with a nod from our hero said hop in. Later he wondered: What ever became of his desert queen?

He was sitting in a cafe in Sedona, Arizona, when a limo arrived with an entourage of security. Out stepped everyman's hero, Arizona Senator John McCain. For a lingering moment he allowed his intellectual curiosity to roam. The old question: If you could stop the monster before he became the monster, would you do it? In the age of cell phone television you could alter history with an awkward moment. Cause him to lose balance. A moment of rage captured for posterity.

He quietly asked no one in particularly: What was so wrong with Ho Chi Minh anyway? The muscles in the broad round neck of America's hero tightened, his veins bulged as he visibly struggled not to look in our hero's direction. He looked around to see if anyone had a cell phone. Maybe. You can never tell. He might have altered history. Then again America's hero looked like he was down for the count. America's hero had loser written all over him. He finished his latte, crawled in his car and drove away.

A million thoughts zigzagged through his head and he discovered a calming comfort in random chaos. Windows down and the desert heat permeating a cool breeze, he wondered why the random accelerator particle collider was considered random. If it was truly random the results would be meaningless and anything, including an all-consuming black hole, would be possible. Just a thought he thought while driving nowhere fast.

He noticed them in a flashing image bounced off the rearview mirror: Two men in dark shades and dark suits, sitting side by side in a nondescript gray Chrysler, not the kind to be driving a barren road into the Nevada desert. Something was up.

Was this the good Senator's work? Was that stodgy old

fart so uptight that he would summon the feds for a crack in the local Starbuck's? He noticed the cell phone embedded in the dash of his 64 Dodge van (they don't make 'em like that any more) and rang up the boys.

"Got some smoke in my mirror, boys, need some roadside assistance."

Like magic he watched the scene unfold a few miles down the road. An accident, people laid out on the pavement, red lights flashing, people in uniforms. They let him pass but stopped the intruders at the gate.

"Somebody up there likes me," he thought.

The highway was free and clear for a hundred miles. The scent of sage and a melting landscape conjured images of ancient lands uninhabited by man. He pulled into a roadside café, wondering how they made a living in such a forsaken place. Must be a front. Had to be a front. Something was going on under the hood.

The waitress was thin and oddly attractive with her painted eyes and ratted blonde hair. She asked him what was up with a wink that seemed incongruous. She was emitting some aroma that made him think of the late sixties, free love and plentiful picnics.

He ordered a cheeseburger without the beef. She laughed and gave him a grilled cheese sandwich and an order of fries on the house. There was no cook in the kitchen, no dishwasher, no one but the woman with ratted hair.

She sat down across the counter while he ate, pouring coffee, batting her eyes, waiting for some sign of interest. He asked her how she managed and she replied not well, pointing to a picture on the wall of a large man in front of a big rig named the Silver Bullet. He went on a run six months ago and never came back. She was minding the store and biding her time, waiting for an opportunity to adventure.

"Where you headed, stranger?"

He told her he was on the road to nowhere, apologizing for the cliché, looking to discover the undercurrents of native life. The grilled cheese was delicious. She undid the top button of her white cotton blouse. The fries were excellent for the frozen variety. She poured some catsup and joined him. Leaning over the counter his eyes traced the outline of her finely tuned breasts. She locked the door, turned over the closed sign and poured a couple of beers.

"No license," she explained.

They drank and told stories about life, husbands, wives, families and twists of fate. He did not believe in fate but she did. It was fate that brought them together in this isolated place on the outskirts of nowhere. She opened her legs and he took her then and there on a revolving counter stool with the scent of fries and the rattle of dishes hovering about them.

She asked him if he wanted to stay and he asked her if she wanted to go. A six pack and an hour later they hit the road, headed for Las Vegas, the city of neon, games of chance, random adventures, strippers and hustlers, cheap thrills and costly addictions. They drove through the barren sage littered landscape smelling of half-baked reptilian remains looking like the dream of a cracker without a clue, talking in seamless cycles on parallel plains that never touch.

Periodically, he took a moment to look at her and nod. She did the same. It was not the reality of connection that mattered but the formality, the courtesy, the habit that gave mythology its teeth.

If he had been listening he would not have understood even a fraction of what she said but the rhythm of her voice was somehow pleasing. If he had been able to decode the message beneath a stream of sounds he would have understood that she was a gentle compassionate woman stuck in the particle collider of a troubled past. She rewound the dialogues that she perceived as keys to the mystery. She dissected decisions that led to wrong choices and guided her on the wrong path. She wondered what she could have done to deserve so little joy and so much sorrow.

He was stuck in the moment or rather a conglomeration

of moments surrounding his present circumstance. His memory could only reach back so far and the incident at the Sedona Starbuck's was as far as it reached. He kept coming back to the incredible arrogance and petty mindedness of the man who wanted to lead the world in war.

On their way to the desk at the Bellagio he plugged a silver dollar into a glittering machine, cashed out and handed it to his companion. They checked into a room on the thirteenth floor and enjoyed an evening of varied entertainment, replete with gambling, music, fine food and sensual exploration. In the morning he got up early, kissed her gently and let her sleep. He left her cash, a credit card, keys to the van and his deed to a house in Malibu. He had pressing business.

He picked up a copy of the Times, booked a flight to the nation's capitol and caught a cab to the airport. On the ride over he felt a seizing of his heart and wondered if he would ever see her again. Hers was a giving spirit, a generous heart, and the feel of her limbs rubbing against his eased his yearning. He gazed out the window at a passing ambulance as it turned into the entryway of a local hospital. He hated hospitals. He had nothing against doctors and nurses. There were good and bad in every profession. But he felt in his gut that hospitals were cesspools of greed and disease.

He breathed in and out, a slow and measured pattern, until he sensed strength returning to his life and limbs, and contemplated the road ahead.

Joe the orderly reported to work every day with his bag lunch and green uniform checking in at the front desk, flirting with the nurses and taking the elevator ride to the twenty-seventh floor. That was where they kept the hard cases, the hopeless, the unfortunate ones whose lives were sustained by machines, breathing machines, blood machines and monitoring devices around the clock until the insurance money ran out.

Despite the downturn in the economy (or perhaps because of it) there was no shortage of customers. It was not difficult for doctors and hospital administrators to convince loved ones, husbands and wives, parents and caretakers, that there was still a glimmer of hope when in fact it was a shot in the dark, one in a billion, the approximate odds of finding a diamond in a trash bin.

Joe did the dirty work, moving from room to room, avoiding rare visitors, changing sheets and bedpans, making sure the tubes were in place and the machines were operating. As he worked it was his habit to change the channels of the overhead televisions, which were invariably set to late night movies, heavy on the soft porn, by the overnight staff. He made an effort to judge what the patient might enjoy in the event that any of it seeped into the subconscious mind, usually settling on cable news or generic music stations.

As he made his rounds he caught the nurse in room 2736 making some adjustments to the patient's medications and cleaning his body with a wet towel. Her name was Bonnie and she was dangerously cute. The patient, an older man and a recent addition to the ward, had an obvious erection beneath his hospital gown. It was not uncommon for unconscious men and Joe wondered if it meant something really was going on in the minds of these patients.

"Why not ease his suffering?" he asked the nurse.

"Why don't you?" she countered.

She told him about the patient. He was a businessman who choked on a giant shrimp while watching a sporting event in his apartment. He was alone and managed to call 911 but the ambulance arrived too late. He had a living will but left no instructions on what to do in the event of incapacity. His wife and family had no clue so after six months in a coma he was transferred to the 27th floor.

He changed the channel to MSNBC and sat waiting for her to finish up.

"What do you make of that?" he asked pointing to the patient's still engorged member.

She said the common view was that it was nothing more than an autonomic response. Conscious men think of sex around the clock because their unconscious minds are wired to procreation to leave their mark on the gene pool. Unconscious men still have the instinct even if their minds are not intact.

"Is that what you think?" he wondered.

She shrugged. She had noticed that some men responded to the sounds of sex on television and some responded to a woman's touch differently than to a man's – unless of course they were attracted to the same sex. The talk was making her a little uncomfortable but she let her gaze linger on the patient's erection before she left with a wink at Joe who was concealing the beginning stages of his own arousal.

Later at break time, they worked the conversation around to the same subject. Nurse Bonnie finally admitted that if it was entirely up to her she would consider it therapeutic to relieve the patient of his pent up sexual frustration but it was not. She could lose her job and anyway no one really knew what if anything was going on inside the patient's head.

Joe smiled at her with genuine good will and told her that if he ended up unconscious in a hospital bed, he would be pleased to be cared for by a nurse as compassionate as she was. That seemed to please her – enough so that later that evening they would make a date for the weekend. It was the beginning of a beautiful relationship in which Joe the orderly's pent up frustration was regularly relieved by the tender attentions of Nurse Bonnie.

They met every night in room 2736 and sometimes their relationship went beyond the bounds of their profession. One night with a full moon shining through an open window, Nurse Bonnie asked Joe to wait outside and let her know if anyone was approaching.

She leaned over and whispered in her patient's ear: I

don't know if you can hear me or whether you understand but if you can I want to help you. If you're suffering, I want to ease your suffering. I want to comfort you. If I do anything that makes you feel uncomfortable, it's up to you to stop me.

The patient did not respond in any recognizable way but it seemed to Nurse Bonnie that his erection was even more pronounced than usual. She wondered if her words, the touch of her breath or the sound of her voice aroused him.

Keeping her head by his, her ear tuned to his voice, she reached down and slowly, gently took hold of his erection. She thought she heard him moan. She could not be sure; it was so soft it was beyond normal perception. She slowly, gently moved her hand up and down, up and down, and she heard his breathing grow slightly stronger.

She ran her fingers through his hair, kissed him on his forehead and stroked his erection until he came. She could not sure but she thought he sighed. She thought he thanked her in the only way he could.

She cleaned his body with a wet towel and called Joe in to help change the sheets. Joe nodded his approval, gave her a hug and a kiss, and then pointed to the patient who seemed to be smiling.

From that day forward, at least once a week, with Joe standing guard at the door, Nurse Bonnie would ease the patient's suffering and celebrate the healing power of her touch.

He took a cab from the airport, picked up a copy of the Post, booked a suite at the Four Seasons and started running up a tab with room service. He bought six executive box tickets to the Redskins game and traded them straight up for two tickets to a production of modern dance at the Kennedy Center for Performing Arts. He ate at the finest restaurants, attended the most elite clubs and hired an escort everywhere he went.

On the third day he approached the concierge with an unusual request: Could he arrange a meeting with someone from the McCain campaign? He folded a couple of crisp one hundred dollar bills in her hand as she indicated that she would see what she could do. Twenty minutes later he received her call in his room. The McCain people were sending a couple of representatives within the hour. She would notify him when they arrived. He thanked her and promised a generous gratuity on his departure.

He had been doing his homework. McCain's main argument against his younger opponent was experience. He knew that the candidate was notoriously prone to rash decisions based on a gut feeling. He wanted to plant a seed in McCain's mind and give him a reason to be rash. A survey of the Republican political landscape yielded one name that would appeal to McCain's vanity and gut instinct and at the same time torpedo his claim of experience: Governor Sarah Palin of Alaska.

She was perfect. She was on the far right, a Christian fundamentalist, and McCain was desperate to please the traditional Republican base. If she had ever expressed an opinion on any issue of national or international importance beyond the sound bites of a political campaign, it was not apparent. She was attractive, confident, ambitious and completely lacking in intellectual curiosity. She was in short George W. Bush in a pretty package – only Bush was better prepared.

The fact that she is a woman would fill McCain with irrational joy, believing that he could steal Hillary Clinton voters on that basis alone. But as the novelty wore off and voters saw her for what she is (a political opportunist) and what she is not (prepared to lead the nation) they would hold McCain responsible for incredibly poor judgment.

When three men in suits showed up at his door, he asked two of them to remain outside. They looked at each other and deferred to the oldest of the three, a man who looked a lot like G. Gordon Liddy of Watergate fame in the Nixon era. Maybe it was Liddy. Who knows? He was here to do the dirty work. No burglary this time, no stealing confidential records for political bribery and extortion, just a little "pay for play."

Before he sat down, he pulled out a small device and swept the room for bugs. It was a clear signal he was prepared for nefarious business. He folded his hands, leaned forward and gazed into our hero's eyes.

"Who are you?" he asked.

"If you don't know that already, you're not doing your job and I'm wasting my time."

"Fair enough," replied Liddy. "What have you got?"

Not what do you want but what have you got. Interesting. He laid it on the table clear and unmistakable. This was a negotiation, a proposal, an exchange of interests like pork bellies for shares in a coal mine. McCain's interest was a pressing need for political contributions. What was he willing to give in return?

"I'm prepared to give six figures on one condition."

He handed Liddy a business card with a name scribbled on the back: Palin.

"The governor of Alaska?"

"That's right. I don't know who's on your list for VP but if it's another old white guy the deal's off. We used to be a party with balls. What have we got now? A washed up warrior, a cross dresser, a Mormon demagogue and a preacher from Arkansas, get serious! Win or lose, the party needs new blood."

Liddy studied the card as if it held the key that would decode a secret message. There was none. It was a straight-up deal. He liked that.

"So you think Governor Palin would give the party balls."

"That's right."

Liddy stood up and shook hands with a tired grin

154

wrinkling his lips.

"I think the old man just might go for it. If he does I'll be in contact."

The man left and our hero contemplated what transpired. It was patently illegal to give a contribution of that size and McCain was supposed to be at the forefront of campaign finance reform. He must be desperate. Even the old money must be tired of Republican policies. They took their profits. Now it was time to restore some balance in the economy before the whole scam broke down. No one wins if the bank goes broke.

He wondered if it was even necessary to pull off this little charade. The McCain campaign was running scared. They would have to win with smoke and mirrors, the same old Republican smear tactics, down and dirty.

Well, he reflected, it worked before. No use taking any chances. He was sure McCain would take the bait. He had played his part. The rest would take care of itself.

He checked out of the hotel, fulfilling his obligation to the concierge, booked a flight to Lisbon and flagged a cab to the airport. He felt a desire for Fado, that centuries old song of mourning and longing from Portugal and the torch singers who embodied it. He wanted to purge his soul. He wanted to be cleansed. He wanted to swim in the sorrows of ancient grief and generations lost and crumbling dreams. He wanted to be reborn in the hope that comes only from shedding his skin.

On the flight across the dark blue sea he felt the forces of gravity, the weight of responsibility, the betrayals of human dignity, the indifference of the powerful, the terrifying coldness of social institutions, the course of history on a troubled, choking planet pushing him to the edge of despair. He closed his eyes and felt the breath of someone gentle and sweet caressing his neck, whispering in his ear.

He awakened refreshed, renewed and invigorated as the

plane descended on the European continent, the birthplace of capitalism and socialism, democracy and fascism, equality and aristocracy, feudalism and the rights of labor, the land of a trillion contradictions in perpetual shades of gray, the shadow hovering over America and much of the modern world.

He checked into a hotel, ordered room service and a hotel computer and wrote for three days. It was the kind of thing he always wanted to do but there was always someone to tell him not to, that the world was waiting, that you could not shut yourself away. It was an indulgence and now he was free to indulge.

He sent it out on the web and forgot about it. The web was the closest thing to a miracle he would ever know. You could send out your words, your thoughts and images, and as long as no one interfered (or even if someone did) they could wander about or sit still for a thousand years only to be discovered at a time and place you could never imagine.

His mind clear and free, he went down to the street and caught a cab to the nearest Fado club. It was a dark place, crowded with men and women of all ages and colors, all yearning and teeming with desire. The crowd hushed, a bright circle of light went up on a small wooden stage, and a singer poured her soul into a story of longing.

She was a beautiful woman, sensuous and strong. She spoke in several languages so everyone in her audience understood the story of each song. Then she sang and grown men choked back tears. Women openly cried and returned the singer's love with praise, a shower of roses and money.

It was an ancient art and it lifted him from time. It relieved him of a multitude of worries, pressures, resentment and regret. He remembered the love, the pain and the sorrow that always lived within his aching heart and then he let them go. He remained in his seat long after most of the patrons had left when she emerged from backstage and cast a smile in his direction.

"Hello, stranger," she said. "You look like you could use some company."

He nodded and she told him of a place where they served fine food and wine at all hours of the night. It was a quiet place where they could talk, drink and feel free to explore the mysteries of existence in a transitory world. He nodded and she guided him there.

They talked to the morning hours and parted as secret lovers only to resume the play of strangers the next evening. On the third night they gave flesh to their affections, swimming in the moonlight of the only love they would ever know. He felt the pull of tomorrow and she released him with a kiss. When two bodies have intermingled as theirs had done they will always be together. They will always be connected. They will always dance in the shadows of the mind. They will always be one.

He carried her scent with him on a train to Madrid to Paris to Berlin to Prague to Amsterdam, breathing in the sights, absorbing the land, the architecture, the ancient ruins, talking by day to familiar souls (an older woman who spoke longingly of deeds undone and dreams unfulfilled, a man whose one remaining wish was redemption, another who revered the love of friends and family), dancing and drinking by night with soulful women whose mystery was as enchanting as their beauty.

He walked along the Seine with a youthful Parisian who promised to remember. He shared an intimate moment in a dark, dank corner of a Bohemian castle with a woman in the Gothic mode. He sipped wine until dawn gazing out a window where the Third Reich once reined in horror with a companion whose empathy was without bound. He danced in the arms of velvet memories where a young Henry Miller and Anais Nin once christened their tortured love in vain. He loved them all and let them go as they did he. As he moved forward he folded his memories behind him in the dark spaces of his mind reserved for treasures. He was a pilgrim on a journey of discovery and such a man can only gaze into the prism of immediacy. There will be time for reflection at the journey's end.

Somewhere outside of Copenhagen he felt the bond of home. It was as if in silence someone was calling his name. It was as if he was living under a spell. He had forgotten who he was and where his seed was sown. It was as if he had bolted from his own life, broke free for as long as he could survive beside himself. He was not lost or disoriented. He knew who he was and he knew where he belonged.

He boarded a plane and flew across the sea, over the top of the world, across the North American continent, and as he flew he dove into the deep waters of unconsciousness for the first time since his journey began. The walls of perception came crashing down. All that he knew was stripped away like flats in an elaborate theatrical production, leaving him naked and alone with his senses.

He was awakened as the plane descended in sweeping spirals to the golden city by the bay. Gazing out his window he grasped the majesty of life on planet earth, the rich textures of land and sea, the smallness of human achievement, the constant flowing motion, wind and rain, roads and traveling souls.

He walked through the bustling airport, people towing luggage and parents towing children, tearful greetings and goodbyes. He walked away from the swarm of activity into the open space outside where he tasted the sweet salt air beneath layers of gasoline, smoke and dust.

He took a cab into the city where he walked the streets crowded with hustling humanity. Men and women minding their business, never stopping to admire the scents of open air cafes, the bite of currents coursing through concrete canyons, never wondering at the generations who built these

158

monuments to human ambition, who sacrificed their lives with the sweat and blood of labor. Couples drinking wine or savoring coffee, heads buried in books, magazines or newspapers, eyes locked to each other, thoughts folded inward while the world rushed by on the other side of a thin veil of glass. They did not hear the orchestra of city life, the purr of motion, the hum of energy, the waves of anxiety and joy carried by the sounds of voices in conversation or decree. They did not see the homeless man on a church's steps, the bag lady and her cart, the street musician or the hustler with a plan. They did not know the miracles unfolding above, below, within and all around.

He found himself outside the Bay View Hospital, no longer tentative, no longer afraid, knowing he had reached the last stage of his journey. Peace had found him. Comfort held him in her arms. Love was waiting.

He lingered in the emergency room where the drama of life and death, of suffering and struggle was raw, clawing at his senses like vinegar on an open wound. He wondered what it would take to ease the pain, knowing from a place deep within that it was all a part of the parade, the journey, the book of knowledge, the growing, the living, the passing, the life. He walked through the afflicted like a shadow of kindness and for a moment the sorrow lifted and the suffering eased. He entered the elevator where an orderly preceded him, pressing the number 27. Glancing at the buttons and looking twice at his fellow traveler, they rose to the twenty-seventh floor and continued in silence to room 2736.

The orderly opened the door and they both walked in: The nurse was listening intently to a visitor, an older woman and her patient's widow. Her face was wet with tears, as she seemed to seek comfort, confirmation or absolution in the decision she had made. The nurse nodded with as much empathy as she could give and nodded again to the orderly who stood back in the corner of the small hospital room, trying to be invisible. He understood what was happening and why he was here. He recognized the woman he loved and the woman who gave her love to him without jealousy or expectation beyond the norms of common decency. He reached out to touch her cheek and felt her shiver. He told her he was fine and he knew she understood. He watched her reach out to touch the patient's cheek and the tears welled in her eyes once more. He held her shoulders and whispered in her ear: *It's time. Let me go.*

She nodded to the nurse who nodded to the orderly and they went about their business of disconnecting life-sustaining devices. She placed her hand on her husband's as he placed his hand on hers and together they watched the dying light of a setting sun.

Somewhere in another part of the world someone was singing:

Vera! Vera! What has become of you?
Does anybody else in here feel the way I do?

It was a song of sorrow and of joy. It was a song of sojourn, of yearning and release. He kissed her three times: One for the past, one for the moment and one for the unknown still ahead.

THE SCENARIO

PART ONE: THE INFORMANT

On the drive to the rendezvous, I tried to visualize what the informant looked like. I pictured an older man with checkered gray hair, full beard, close cut, slightly unkempt, a little fuzzy around the edges. I smiled, realizing I had painted a portrait of my now retired professor of International Studies at Columbia University.

If the informant was what he presented himself to be, it was an inept analogy. The professor had been a dissident voice, a defender of civil liberties and an outspoken advocate of civil disobedience. Rumors persisted that he was forced into retirement in the second wave of antiterrorism legislation. I had wanted to contact him to write his story but I was advised against it. It was easy to rationalize that decision then as now but it left a deep impression of regret.

By contrast, this informant was anything but a dissident. He was an insider, a political operative at best and, quite possibly, a rogue agent, a turncoat to his colleagues and secret ally in the struggle for freedom.

In the space of a few minutes the informant had accomplished what he intended; he established credibility. His cautionary tone, almost indifferent, an air of confidence, the sense that he was offering directives to be followed without question, a game of phone tag leading to a location on the wrong side of town, all combined to convince a skeptical reporter that he was what he claimed to be: the real deal.

I cursed myself for not having insisted on a name or at

least some useful contact. What kind of reporter was I? I was operating on pure speculation and blind faith. It was the kind of situation that invited trouble – as it had before in my tenuous career as a journalist. I swore it would not happen again. It was always the same thing: my weakness, my need and hunger for the story.

I gazed out the window of a yellow cab as we drove past the brownstone towers in one of the poorest neighborhoods in the city, monuments to generations of poverty and a reminder of our government's failure to address it. When was the last time a politician referred to the war on poverty? The problem of the poor had become an assault on the middle class. Like Vietnam and the war on drugs, it was better to forget.

The idea had been to combat crime on the streets, create community pride, and thereby save the urban landscape, but concentrations of poverty in high-rise buildings did not have the desired effect. Crime was more rampant than ever and the towers became markers for urban blight. Like a domestic domino theory the government pressed on with its grand experiment long after its obvious failure. What else could they do?

We drove past the pimps, hookers, junkies, and a cacophony of boom box rap before arriving at the appointed address. It was the basement of an abandoned storefront. I took note of an all night café on the corner across the street before paying the cabbie. At least there was a place I could use to get off the street while waiting for a cab to return me to the relative safety of my middle class apartment.

"Who are you?" I asked.

The informant was nothing like my former professor. He was an older man, clean shaven, white haired and crew cut, his dress informal but meticulous. The general impression was distinctly military. He claimed to be an analyst and spoke of "the agency" in tones bordering reverence. He said that for twenty years his job had been to run scenarios: What if scenarios.

"We took situations, real and hypothetical, and ran them through probability quotients. We analyzed the results and projected outcomes."

Despite my protests, he insisted on beginning his story in Lebanon, Beirut, circa 1983. It was the year a militant group of Shiite Muslims attacked the American Embassy, killing dozens of CIA operatives and capturing the Agency's station chief for Middle East operations. According to the informant, they ran a scenario that indicated any response had to be covert. They were unwilling to risk congressional inquiry.

"Our hands were everywhere. We were supporting both sides in every conflict. We were sponsoring Islamic fundamentalists as a buffer against Soviet influence."

The Reagan Republicans had conspired with America's most hated enemy, Ayatollah Khomeini of Iran, for the release of American hostages immediately after Reagan's inauguration as president. The deal culminated in the delivery of weapons and spare parts in exchange for funds that, in turn, were used to arm the Contras in Nicaragua – expressly forbidden by an act of Congress.

"If ever there was a cause for impeachment," the informant said, "this was it. Reagan consorted with the enemy to defraud an election, openly defied Congress, and lied to cover his tracks. What is the definition of treason if this was not?"

I began to suspect it was either a hoax or a trap. In my years as a reporter, I had seen it all. I once took a shot at the paper's corporate owner, refusing to run stories that were obvious plants, and I had paid for my indiscretions. I was kicked out of the newsroom and given a desk in Metro. I was hoping that this story would give me the jump I needed to get my career back on line but I was losing faith.

"I just don't believe you," I confessed. "I don't believe you were ever with the Agency. I think you're just some radical looking for attention."

"Did I say I was with the Agency?" he replied with a cynical smile. Then he shrugged with an incredulity that was as biting as it was sincere.

"You're right. You found me out."

I was dumfounded. I wanted to be disappointed but what I felt was relief. The journalist within me was dying an awkward death. I had to consider the consequences. I had a wife and child. At least I still had a job. Many did not. At least I still had my freedom.

I clicked off my recorder, gathered my notes and stuffed them in my briefcase. Out of habit, I reached out to shake hands with the man who had just played me for a fool. The informant, with a sardonic pose, placed a business card in my hand: "William Sinclair, Consultant."

"Same time tomorrow?" he asked.

I laughed but felt a rising anger that I knew was fear at its core.

"We'll see," I replied.

I left thinking I would toss his card in the first trashcan I saw.

PART TWO: GRAVITY

I knew someone who knew someone at the Agency. I had contacts at the Pentagon and the State Department. I could make a few calls and tap my sources – or not. I could play the part of a journalist or go back to Metro and be a good boy. Nothing was certain.

I struggled with it through the night, like a shadow at the dinner table, like a ghost in the bed I shared with my faithful wife. I did not confide in her. She would only support me as she had always done. I was a good husband and father. She was a good mother and wife. I did not want her support. I wanted a way out that would allow me to retain some sense of self-esteem. The only way was to see it through.

I made the calls and what I found was conclusive: William Sinclair was the real deal. His involvement with the Agency went back three decades. He had risen from a low level data processor to a prime analyst when suddenly, in 1996, he went AWOL. If the Agency knew why they were not talking. They wanted Sinclair back in their fold and the man who turned him in could expect a sizable reward. I could be the hero of my own story. I could get my desk back in the newsroom. Somewhere in the back of my mind, I still wanted a Pulitzer.

"I knew you'd come," smiled Sinclair.

"The hell you did," I replied.

A man like him leaves nothing to chance. In the vernacular of the intelligence community, he knew more about me than I knew about myself. I wondered: What did he know that made him think I was his boy? Was it a sting? Was it all a part of the domestic offensive in the perpetual war on terrorism? If so, I was vulnerable the moment I walked through the door.

I asked why he had chosen me. He replied that I was not his first choice. He had considered a number of reporters who had shown some backbone, some integrity, some degree of professional pride but none had passed the test.

I soon learned that the test involved enduring Sinclair's lectures on the history of American foreign policy. One of his favorite themes was that Americans have no sense of history. In the world according to Sinclair, that was what distinguished America from the rest of the civilized world.

"To America, Vietnam is ancient history. To the rest of the world, it was only yesterday."

He rambled on about Operation Phoenix in the early stages of the war, when 20,000 South Vietnamese were allegedly rounded up and executed. They were supposed to be our allies. He talked about free fire zones and the commonality of My Lai. He claimed that three million Southeast Asians had lost their lives as the result of our actions.

"We don't count enemy dead," he said with a profound sadness. "There was a time when we did."

He sat behind his naked desk in the sparsely furnished room and stared into space, as if he could still see their faces, their wide dark eyes, their contorted and charred bodies.

"The Vietnamese are the bravest people in world history. After fighting every empire from the Ottoman to the British and French, they turned back the most powerful military force the world has ever seen."

I was moved by his account and wondered what role he had played in the war. It was not my purpose, however, to revisit Vietnam or to rewrite history according to one rogue agent. When I said as much, Sinclair poured a large glass of water and dropped it on the concrete floor, shards of glass scattering like shrapnel from an antipersonnel bomb.

"What is this?" he challenged.

"An irrational display of self righteous indignation," I replied. He had already been through any number of reporters. I was confident he needed me as much as I needed him.

"Gravity," he answered. "Come back when you have some sense of it."

I went home and did some homework.

PART THREE: HISTORY

Sinclair's history lesson resumed with Nicaragua in the early eighties. The Agency backed the Contras, a ruthless paramilitary force, against the Sandinistas, a coalition of working class and indigenous peoples. It was there that an infamous Agency Operations Manual was uncovered.

As Sinclair put it: "How to Subvert Popular Government by Terrorist Tactics."

It openly advocated a nightmare scenario: Creating an atmosphere of constant fear with random looting, rape and murder, techniques of torture, hiring criminals to do the dirty work, assassination, and creating martyrs by killing your own leaders. He added that the Agency would not hesitate to use the same tactics within our own country if it believed it could get away with it. He connected the dots: Nixon and Watergate, Reagan and Iran-Contra, Malcolm X, the Black Panthers, the Kennedy assassinations and Martin Luther King.

I was reluctant to consider such a wide brush for any story in the current political climate. The mere whisper of conspiracy, past, present or future, would never get past the editorial board of any major news organization, including mine. Still, he left an impression, almost unthinkable thoughts, unspeakable possibilities that would transform my dreams to nightmares and darken my view of the world for years to come. It was not the world I believed in. It was not the world I wanted to believe in. I was not prepared to accept such a radical transformation of reality.

Sinclair went on about our involvements throughout Latin America: El Salvador, Guatemala, Chile, Grenada, Panama, Columbia, Argentina, Bolivia and Peru. (In Argentina, 9-11 recalls the Agency sponsored coup that replaced Salvador Allende with the butcher Augusto Pinochet.) Everywhere it was the same story: Subversion of lawful democracies in favor of military despots. We allied ourselves with thugs, criminals and drug lords.

He lingered on the story of Archbishop Oscar Romero, a clergyman who stood up against oppression of the poor. It was hardly noted in the American press when nearly 200,000 peasants were slaughtered in Guatemala, but when six Jesuit priests, four American missionaries and Archbishop Romero were tortured and executed, it was front-page news.

"Why do they hate us?" he asked with a twisted grin.

"They hate us for Suharto, America's bloody gift to Indonesia. They hate us for the massacre of East Timor, where the price of opposition was one quarter of their population.

"Why do they hate us?"

He was pacing the room, gaining momentum, as he moved on to the Middle East: Iran, Iraq, and Afghanistan. The first Gulf War was fought over the issues of cross-drilling and Kuwaiti belligerence. Saddam Hussein cleared the invasion with the American consulate but he could not have been surprised by America's betrayal. It was an opportunity to establish dominance in a critical region. Our objective was accomplished when we refused to leave as promised after the war.

"Why do they hate us? We financed Islamic militants throughout the world but especially in Afghanistan when the Soviets invaded. After the Russians pulled out, we asked our 'freedom fighters' to return our more sophisticated weaponry. They politely declined."

If it was an argument, Sinclair was winning. My mind was opening to the possibility that our government was guilty of massive crimes against humanity. I was beginning to believe that we – our government, our intelligence forces, and our military – were the real terrorists but my mind stopped short, unable to make that leap.

I wondered why he left the Agency. He had known these things for years. Why would he continue to work for an agency that was at least partly responsible for so much suffering and death? It was not something he wanted to address. His eyes grew cold; his entire body seemed to shrivel like an old man in a storm. Finally, he produced an obituary and quietly sat down while I read:

"William Randolph Sinclair, Jr., 27, of Arlington, VA, died at St. Jude's Medical Center. He was a veteran of Desert Storm. He is survived by...." The pieces started falling into place. His son, following the example of his father, lost his life in consequence.

"You wrote a story," said Sinclair, "about the Gulf War Syndrome. Remember?"

I had indeed. As many as half of the soldiers who served in the first war later contracted the sickness. It began with a mild rash, headaches, nausea, but developed into a neurological disorder resembling Parkinson Disease. Whatever the cause – depleted uranium munitions, experimental vaccines – the military chose to deny its existence rather than investigate and face the consequences. When they were forced to investigate, their findings were always inconclusive.

"Billy walked over to the high school football field," continued Sinclair. "He was a star athlete, you know. He walked out into the center of the field, knelt as if in prayer, and put the barrel of a shotgun in his mouth...." His face grew ever darker and a shadow seemed to come over him. His gaze went inward as he summoned the image of his child.

"Before Billy died it was just a game. Not any more."

The history lessons were over. It was not that I had won his trust. It was just that he no longer seemed to care. If his story had merit and I had the courage to run with it, it was mine.

PART FOUR: THE SCENARIO

Sinclair came up with the terrorist attack scenario in January 1996, ten months before his son ended his own life. It proposed a simultaneous attack by an Islamic fundamentalist group on several cities within the United States. It was an attack on both civilian and government targets – the Washington Monument, Disney World, the World Trade Center, the Pentagon – using commercial airlines as missiles. His superiors were intrigued and asked him to give the enemy a name. He did so. The name had been around for years and his face was that of the perfect enemy: Usama bin Laden. He emphasized that none of this was the product of his imagination.

"I have no imagination," he said. "I wasn't a fiction writer. I was not paid to write stories. I was paid to create realistic scenarios based on existing facts. Everything is in the public record."

He instructed me to check the official transcripts from the investigations of the African embassy bombings, the attack on the USS Cole and the trial records of the first attack on the World Trade Center. I did so. It all checked out. Usama bin Laden, altered after September 11, 2001, to Osama bin Laden was an Agency recruit from the days of the Soviet invasion of Afghanistan.

Sinclair explained that he ran a cost-benefit analysis, projecting the cost in lives and economic loss against the "benefits" to the Agency and the powers it served: Increased military spending, congressional approval of covert operations, broad powers of domestic surveillance, control of Congress and the White House, and, most critically, a forty year "war on terrorism" – a long awaited replacement for the Cold War. It would be a virtual carte blanche for the neoconservative ideologues already entrenched in the White House.

"It would have been so easy to prevent this catastrophe," he said. He reminded me that the director of the Federal Aviation Administration pleaded with Congress and the administration to secure the cockpits of commercial airlines long before September 2001.

"Where was the Agency then?" he asked. "Where was the FBI? Where were all those men in high office who knew what was being planned and did nothing to prevent it? It would have been so easy."

I had always considered myself a good, patriotic citizen. Even if I did not always agree with my government, I believed my country was the best and most virtuous on the planet. This was not a story I wanted to hear, no less report: That our leaders – those in charge of defending our nation – knew what was about to happen and failed to act.

Sinclair offered me an envelope. He explained that it contained all the evidence I would require. I hesitated. I imagined he was reading my mind: Was this really what I wanted? Did I wish to go down in history as the man who exposed the great lie? Did the facts even matter? Would I be vilified by my colleagues in the press? Would I be called a traitor? Would I lose my job and everything I valued and worked so hard to protect?

I took the envelope in my hands, held it for the length of a second thought, and tossed it onto Sinclair's desk. I had a confession to make. I had already contacted the authorities.

"I suspect," I said, "there are a couple of agents outside right now."

Sinclair flashed his sardonic smile.

"Congratulations," he said. "You passed the test."

I looked at him with disbelief. All of his passion and conviction were nothing but smoke and mirrors, lies and deceptions, like the lies of war.

"You try to convince me that my government has betrayed the nation, its people, its founding principles, and if you succeed, I go to jail."

"You want to work in the fourth estate," he replied, "that's the test. It's the price you pay to enjoy the blessings of your profession and the esteem, the privilege and the power of serving the greatest nation on earth."

He was wrong. The price was much greater. Beneath his twisted sense of humor, a profound sadness would stay with us both as long as we lived. For each of us, shame was the price of survival.

He winked and I went my way. I was back in the newsroom. A few months later, I was given a column and a seat on the editorial board. I never asked my publisher if he was in on the sting. I never had to. It was understood.

BORDERS

Johansen was six years past three quarters of a century old. Despite a lifelong respect for science and logic he had an affinity for all things poetic and mystical – including numerology. The number nine is a symbol of destiny and finality and no destiny is more final than the undiscovered country he envisioned for his eighty first year on earth.

"Well, my friend," he said as he stuffed a bag of trail mix into his travel bag, "I've come to a decision."

His friend, McGhee, just shook his head and smiled. He knew full well what Johansen's decision would be.

"I'm an old man," said Johansen. "My eyes are fading. My ears no longer hear the subtleties of music. My touch is coarse and brittle. My taste? Well, the most exquisite meal might as well be a McDonald's fish sandwich. My knees have a marked tendency to buckle at the most inopportune times. In short, what good am I?"

"You're a great deal of good to any man that knows you," offered McGhee.

"And the women?"

"The women, too."

"You're too kind. And you make my point."

The point was that everyone Johansen had ever known was already dead or close enough that it no longer seemed to matter. He had given up the numbing process of watching his friends die. The first part was accepting that they no longer were themselves. The hardest part was remembering that what they had become was still connected to what they used to be. He had sworn he would never visit that haunting phase where only death awaits like an interminable tease.

The wind whistled a gentle lullaby, a soft supple motion of soothing melodic calm. He sat rocking on his porch overlooking the rocky fields of tall grass. It was early fall – plenty of time for a final march to the sea.

"I've decided to make an end."

"Nonsense," said McGhee. "You've plenty of good work in you."

"Maybe. But I'm tired of work and I've lost my feel for play. I should have been a poet and a flute player. I should never have become a useful human being."

"Where's your religious upbringing, man?" replied McGhee. "You cannot take these things into your own hands. You'll send yourself straight to hell!"

"Not even you believe that."

McGhee shook his head with a wry grin. It was almost as though he was alive. But old Mac had gone to the great wonder years ago. Johansen kept him around because he was the only one who could still amuse him. For years, McGhee had been the only one who endured Johansen.

"Well, since you're determined, what exactly did you have in mind?"

"You know exactly what I have in mind," said Johansen. "Haven't you watched me planning, scheming, debating, philosophizing all these many years? Isn't it time you figured out what exactly I had in mind?"

"There's a lot of clutter in that mind of yours," said McGhee. "So if you don't mind, give it to me straight and simple."

"My bag is packed," said Johansen. "I've got everything I need. I'm going to get up at the crack of dawn and march to the sea."

"Are you cracked, man?"

"Not quite. But I'm one good fall away from it."

"It's a long walk."

"I've got my walking stick. I'll make my way."

"There's two, maybe three border crossings between here

and there. They'll never let you cross."

"I've the perfect solution to that problem," said Johansen. He pulled a set of wire cutters out of his bag and smiled. He would go the back way, across the fields and meadows, never having to deal with the border guards.

"My god," said McGhee, "you are cracked."

Johansen smiled and allowed himself the pleasure of reminiscence. He could not count the years since he had seen, heard, touched and tasted the sweet scent of his first and greatest love: the sea. He loved the stark, biting air, the scent of fresh dried seaweed, the flight of the gulls and the special class of the human race that inevitably answered her siren's song. Most of all he loved her vastness, her impenetrable mystery, her sacred promise of a destiny beyond reckoning, as infinite and immovable as the stars.

"I should have been a sailor," he said wistfully.

"You were a sailor!" replied McGhee.

"I was a fisherman," said Johansen. "They're not the same thing."

"The sea is the sea," said McGhee.

"How wrong you are, my friend." He sighed and listened to the breeze whispering memories. "That was before we fished her clean. The tuna, the mackerel, the marlin, the squid and the lobster: All gone. Which is why I am what I am today."

"The finest handyman I ever knowed."

"Yes. And what good is that?"

Johansen shuffled inside, hunched shoulders and lost in a myriad of thoughts, where he forced himself to consume a meal of biscuits and gravy washed down with a bucket of ale.

In the morning, he had a light breakfast and began the long walk. The air was crisp and full of wonder. He gloried at the sight of butterflies, a lone fox on a far bluff, who seem puzzled by the strange visitor to his kingdom of open fields, and bold seagulls venturing inland just to say hello. If Johansen had ever felt more alive, he could not remember when.

It was difficult cutting through the barbed wire fencing, set up by the border patrol to dissuade just such excursions, but he managed it in the measured, steady manner of a man with fortitude and determination. As the first day ended, flush with exhaustion, he lay beneath the open skies, spotted with more stars than his aged eyes could grasp, and praised the glories of nature and the majesty of mother earth.

He was awakened by the sound of what he thought was a monstrous heartbeat. He opened his eyes to see a large gray helicopter whisking away, the words "Border Patrol" still visible on its side.

"You've had it now," said McGhee. "They've spotted you."

Johansen cursed the air and thought about scouting a hiding post. But he knew his friend was right. He'd been spotted. There was nothing to do but wait for the guards to haul him away to the nearest border crossing station.

"Idiot!" he said aloud. He had made no plans for this contingency. He was so far removed from the trodden path that it did not occur to him that they still patrolled these vast open spaces by air.

"Johansen, is it?" said the guard as he scattered the contents of his travel bag on a bare wooden table. His eyes were immediately drawn to the mixture of potions he had devised for his last goodnight. "Idiot," he said to himself as the guard opened the medicine bottle and gave it a sniff. He ought to have buried it the moment he was spotted. Possession of such substances had long been forbidden. It was grounds for indefinite detention.

"Well, well," said the guard.

Johansen explained that it was strictly medicinal, a potion designed for his own peculiar infirmities. His tone and demeanor were so sincere that he almost convinced the young guard before McGhee intervened with a comment of his own: "And if you believe that then I'm the Pope and my friend here is the Virgin Mary."

Unfortunately, as happened time and again, McGhee's words popped out of Johansen's mouth before he had time to catch them. Johansen would be held in a detention cell until the contents of the potion could be analyzed. Then they would decide whether to send him home or take harsher measures.

There was a time when the border crossing detention centers were filled with the wandering homeless. By now even the despondent had learned it was nearly impossible to cross the borders without proper documentation. So Johansen was alone in his cell except for his imaginary friend. Having calculated that he was solely to blame, McGhee was forlorn and cried like a babe until Johansen wished him away.

He cursed the world for having created these border crossings out of fear and intolerance. He cursed the government for cutting up the land into patrol sections and making prisons of the towns and villages where people lived. He cursed the media for packaging and selling fear – fear of crime, fear of terrorists, fear of immigration, fear of disease, fear of religion, fear of economic collapse – as if it was a highly valued commodity. He cursed the people for their credulity, for allowing the Great Reform to sweep across the globe, for exchanging their freedom for the false promise of security.

He then lay down on his cot, closed his eyes and summoned the goddess of the sea. She came to him with the sweet music of her constant motion, her eternal grace. She enfolded him in her arms and placed him on a high cliff overlooking her endless mystery. She sang to him in songs familiar and new, a serenade to his undying spirit and love of all things beautiful. He answered her siren's song one last time and she welcomed him as a long lost child.

In the morning, the guard found in his cell a motionless

old man with hunched shoulders and a smile of sweet remembrance painted on his face. The guard tried to rouse him without success. Johansen was no longer there. He was far, far away in the undiscovered country of his dreams.

ABOUT THE AUTHOR

Jack Random has lived at once an ordinary and extraordinary life. His roots firmly planted in the fertile central valley of California, he has marched the streets in protest, haunted jazz town bars, read poetry in cafes and town squares, strutted his hour upon the stage, crisscrossed the country by air, rail, highway and thumb, mourned at Wounded Knee, gazed into the eyes of the crow at Grand Canyon, and paid tribute at the grave of Geronimo. He has labored in the fields of plenty, toiled on the assembly line, pursued higher education and attempted to enlighten children in the public schools. He has been a pilgrim and a seeker of truth. He is married to the love of his life. All the while he has chronicled his thoughts and revelations in words: plays, poetry, novels, stories and essays. His first novel *Ghost Dance Insurrection* (Jazzman Series) was originally published by Dry Bones Press (2000).

OTHER BOOKS FROM CROW DOG PRESS

Wasichu: The Killing Spirit – A Novel by Jack Random. A modern day telling of the life of Crazy Horse recalls the history of Native America and its most revered leader.

Number Nine: The Adventures of Jake Jones and Ruby Daulton – A Novel by Jack Random. A woman on the run picks up a hitchhiker and takes us on an adventure that winds its way to New Orleans in the summer of Katrina.

A Patriot Dirge – A Novel by Jack Random. Political genius Roman Mason takes on the political and economic forces that rule our lives (Jazzman Series).

Jazzman Chronicles: Volumes I–X – Essays by Jack Random. Political commentaries from 2000 to 2014.

A Mother's Story – Stories, Art and Reflections by Artis Brown Miller. A mother of eight children reflects on a life of hardship and love.

Pawns to Players: The Stairway Scandal – A Novel by Jack Random. An aristocrat and a billionaire play a chess match to determine the fate of the American government.

Pawns to Players: A Match for the White House – A Novel by Jack Random.

The Grand Canyon Zen Golf Tour – A Memoir by Jack Random. Two friends embark on a journey of golf, music, poetry and family in the summer of 1993.

Apache Jack: Native Visions & Stories by Jack Random. A collection of short works including *Desert Dreams*.

www.ingramcontent.com/pod-product-compliance
Lightning Source LLC
Chambersburg PA
CBHW021152130626
46554CB00005B/1776